COLLECTING RUSSIAN ART & ANTIQUES

COLLECTING RUSSIAN ART & ANTIQUES

Marina Bowater

HIPPOCRENE BOOKS
New York

For information, address:
HIPPOCRENE BOOKS, INC.
171 Madison Avenue
New York, NY 10016

Library of Congress Cataloging-in-Publication Data
Collecting Russian art & antiques / Marina Bowater.
p.   cm.
Includes bibliographic references
ISBN 0-87052-897-1(hbk)
ISBN 0-87052-142-X (pbk)
1. Art, Russian—Collectors and collecting.
I. Title.
II. Title: Collecting Russian art and antiques.
N6981. B69   1990
709'.47'075—dc20   90-22076
CIP

*For Major General John Bowring
and his wife, Iona.*

Contents

TRANSLITERATION

Sometimes transliteration of Russian names into English confuses the lay reader, but, in general, the rules for it as laid down by the Library of Congress have been adhered to in this book. Tsars' names are presented mainly in English form; most other names are rendered in the Russian manner.

RUSSIAN RULERS FROM IVAN III

Ivan III	1462–1505
Basil IV	1505–1533
Ivan IV	1533–1584
Fedor I	1584–1598
Boris Godunov	1598–1605
Fedor II	1605–
Time of Troubles (inter-regnum)	1605–1613
Michael	1613–1645
Alexis	1645–1676
Fedor III	1676–1682
Sophia (regent)	1682–1689
Ivan V (co-tsar)	1682–1689
Peter I (co-tsar)	1682–1689
Peter I (sole tsardom/*samoderjhavetz)*	1689–1725
Catherine I	1725–1727
Peter II	1627–1730
Anna Ioanovna	1730–1740
Ivan VI	1740–1741
Anna Leopoldovna (Regent)	1740-1741
Elizabeth	1741–1762
Peter III	1762 (6 months)

Catherine II	1762–1796
Paul	1796–1801
Alexander I	1801–1825
Nicholas I	1825–1855
Alexander II	1855–1881
Alexander III	1881–1894
Nicholas II	1894–1917
Provisional Government (March–November)	1917
Bolshevik Revolution (November 6-Old Style / October 24-New Style)	1917
Treaty of Brest Litovsk (December 15)	1917

Russian Hall-marks.

1. Hall-mark of year 7194 from the creation of the world (1686). 2. Hall-mark of the year 7206 from the creation of the world (1698). 3. Hall-mark of grade; seventeenth century. 4. Mark denoting Imperial ownership (seventeenth century). 5. Mark denoting the object to be in the possession of the Patriarchal Treasury. 6. Local hall-mark: Moscow. 7. Local hall-mark: Irkutsk. 8. Local hall-mark: Kazan. 9. Local hall-mark: Kostroma. 10. Hall-mark of Moscow. 11. Hall-mark of St. Petersburg. 12. Inspectors' mark with date. 13. Local hall-mark (St. Petersburg) with date. 14. Local hall-mark (Moscow) with date. 15. Maker's mark. 16. Grade indication. (*Courtesy Tamara Talbot Rice*)

Foreword

Writing on the subject of collecting the arts of Imperial Russia presents an author with immense problems—the main one being that the Western world knows so little about the Soviet Union. Few English speaking peoples realize that Russia's latter-day development, paradoxically, was much like that of the United States of America: the Russian Empire pushed out to the East as America did to the West. Russia colonized Siberia, Kazakstan and other wild and undeveloped lands, including the Caucasus, predominently in the nineteenth century. America's Louisiana Purchase and the incorporation of the Spanish far-western lands (California, for instance) also took place in that exciting century.

It is necessary for a collector to have knowledge of the culture in order to appreciate the significance of the artifacts. Assuming, as I must, that the reader knows very little about Russia, I have structured this book to include an in-depth picture of the manner in which each collectible object developed through the centuries against the backdrop of the country's historical and political progress. Each chapter is devoted to one type of artifact from its inception. I include the characteristics which help to determine authenticity of an object as well as clues concerning where to find it outside its country of origin.

A tall order, but a delightful one because the arts of Russia are often unique, colorful and different. Space necessitates that I concentrate on collectibles; architecture, music, the stage and its customs are not fully discussed in this work. The portable items of Russian production, however are of the greatest interest.

I have concluded this book with a chapter on the arts of the post-1917 revolutionary era since they are the reflections of Russia's dazzling, if turbulent, past. They too can be found on the commercial markets of the West, although with greater difficulty in view of political and geophysical problems.

—M.B.

The Cinderella of the Arts

*C*ollectors and dealers can be said to be one and the same, for most collectors deal and most dealers collect. They are both driven by the same force—the element of the chase that exists in searching for and finding the things that are of specific interest. The tracking down of items, however, is much easier when little or nothing is known about them, as it is in the case of Russian art, for this enables the knowledgeable collector to make a find. But such days are fading fast.

Specialized knowledge, self-confidence and a certain instinct play a significant role in such hunting, particularly when goods are bought outside auction rooms where most objects are identified and described by experts, although inevitably occasional mistakes are made. For the small collector or the beginner, the answer lies in entering into congenial relations with a reputable dealer, or dealers, from whom knowledge can be gleaned and the beginnings of a collection can be established safely; the self-conducted hunt can come later. Regular attendance at auction sales is also recommended since this is the best way to establish familiarity with current market prices.

For the collection of Russian art difficulties abound. The identifying marks on porcelain, for example, must be learned for they are mostly in Cyrillic; the characteristics of the ethnic china dolls called *koulaki* must be recognized for what they are because the dolls are not always stamped with identifying marks. Anyone interested in icons, silver, malachite and pictorial art from the pre-and post-revolutionary periods should do some reading before investing. But then, again, not every successful collector has done the reading beforehand.

A major problem that confronts collector and dealer alike are the fakes which are encountered all too often these days in every field of the arts— the Russian icon being most often suspect. All of which underwrites the fact that an indepth study of the subject should always be made before attempts at the serious assembly of a collection, or of an investment. "Gorby's Gremlins," by which name the fakes that arrive from the Soviet Union are generally referred to today, are very often quite spendid. But the guilty party is not always the Soviet Union. The writer once saw a magnificent collection of porcelain Easter eggs in all colors of the rainbow, all of which bore the personal crowned cypher in gold relief of Russia's Empress Dowager, Maria Fedorovna. They were presented in a Fabergé-style, holly box, on the base of which was the label someone had forgotten to remove: Made in Japan.

The West's tremendous interest in Russian art generated during the past few decades has intensified due to *glasnost,* and is a phenomenon of interesting dimensions. It is an interest which could stand some investigation, and to do so a brief excursion should be made into the country's past.

Curtains of various textures have separated western and eastern Europe for many centuries, including the present one of iron which, hopefully, is corroding. So, little is known of Russia, let alone her arts. Russia had no Renaissance as was enjoyed by the West, due to the barbarous occupation of her central and southern regions by the Golden Horde (a Tartar/

Mongol alliance), which was not dispersed until the mid-sixteenth century. During those several centuries of penurious occupation the one true form of artistic expression that existed in Russia was iconography, which grew to become an artform of the first magnitude.

The accession of Peter the Great (b.1672, sole tsardom 1689–1725), marked an indelible line of change across every aspect of the country's endeavours. But it was in the reign of his youngest daughter, Elizabeth, that art really came into its own.

Although the arts blossomed into a veritable Russian Renaissance under her influence, her country's art forms were not brought seriously to the West's attention until the early years of this century. It was that impressario of larger–than–life dimension, Sergei Pavlovich Diaghilev, who finally introduced them to the west.

There exists a certain attraction to many of these Russian arts, whichever form they take, that enhances interest in their origins, for they possess their own essential vitality, distinct sense of movement and color (especially the icons which were the central element of Russian culture), and frequently a story exists about their initial creation.

One such story emanates from the depths of the Ural mountain range, in Siberia, where a golden goddess called Jumala existed. Her idol was made from solid gold and had another idol within it, and inside that, another, and when the wind passed through it the figure appeared to sing. Her cult is said to exist to this day in the more remote, taiga regions of Siberia. Derivations of her cult are the small, highly colored wooden dolls that unscrew to expose another doll within and inside that another. The production of such dolls was banned in medieval Russia by the all-powerful Orthodox Church authorities. They also banned all portrait sculpture in the round, particularly in connection with religious desiderata, to prevent idolatry of the graven image.

In the same manner as the R.S.S.R. (Russian Soviet Socialist Republic) is the largest nation within the U.S.S.R. today, so she was in the Empire of pre-revolutionary Russia, as well as being the dominant one. This, of course, is the reason why, colloquially, the term "Russia" is applied to the multitude of homogeneous countries which constitute the U.S.S.R., for whom she provided the rudiments of civilization in much the same way as England did for her colonies. Collecting Russian artwork and antiques may, therefore, include artifacts which have originated in locations geographically at great distances from each other. This, too, is the reason why Russian art is so often accused by historians of being plagiaristic of other cultures to which, invariably, a dash of the Orient is added. The extraneous influences on Russian art, as was the case in all Occidental countries, were due to historical and cultural relationships which were rather different from those in the rest of Europe.

The ninth century saw the Russian Slavs entreat the Norsemen to come and rule over them. The emissaries' astounding offer—"Our land is rich and abundant but has no order. Come, rule over us!"—very quickly brought a response. The Norse prince Rurik was the founder of the first Russian dynasty of consequence. Norse art, however, left only a faint mark for posterity, predominently on carving and pattern, for in the end the Norsemen were themselves Slavonicised. Further self-imposed domination of Russia by the Byzantines (though only in religion and the arts) brought Christianity in 988 A.D., but the Byzantines themselves were not assimilated, though their culture was. The Tartars also ended their suzerainty over Russia with a certain amount of assimilation, hence the saying: "Scratch a Russian and you find a Tartar."

As has been said, it was when Peter the Great finally brought Russia as the great new northern power into cultural competition with the rest of Europe that art was able to spread its wings, to shed the limitations of the past and to enter an era of quite extraordinary progress.

Is Russian art indeed the Cinderella of the arts? Regrettably it must be said that this is so due to all the afore-mentioned reasons. It was not until 1906 that Diaghilev went to Paris to hold preliminary discussions regarding the presentation of the Russian opera and ballet to the Parisians. He took with him a collection of paintings by the greatest of his countrymen, an exhibition which was mounted in the Russian section of the Salon d'Automne at the Grand Palais for which the theatrical decorator Léon

Bakst designed the twelve rooms that housed it. In 1907 Diaghilev presented a series of concerts to French audiences for a first time, and in 1908 arranged for the performance of Mussorgsky's *Boris Godunov* at the Paris Opera, with Chaliapin singing the Tsar's role, supported by the entire St. Petersburg Company. 1909 brought the ballet. This was the beginning—a beginning brought to an abrupt end by the Revolution in 1917. A brief spurt of enthusiasm in the West continued into the 20s through the efforts of Diaghilev's genius, but, with his death in 1929, interest in all things Russian went into decline, other than some considerable attention to the avant-garde movement.

In the years leading up to the Second World War, a gallery that specialized in Russian art was opened in London by Prince Vladimir Galitzine, and proved both interesting and enchanting for collectors. It was a time, of course, when there were plenty of Russian objects to be found due to the unending stream of White Russian refugees, most of whom were in transit to the Americas and were selling the few possessions they had succeeded in salvaging in order to survive.

In Paris there existed a similar emporium called À la Vieille Russie that was run by Léon Grinberg and later others when he moved to New York. The war ended his venture, and it was not until the late 1950s that I (Marina Bowater) followed in their wakes, and opened a similar gallery in London, at a time when the Russian art market was almost unknown.

When I entered the commercial world of art, perhaps naturally in view of my Russian origins, I found myself gravitating towards the artifacts of Imperial Russia. I knew the country's language and history, and I found myself fascinated by the amount of Russian goods that were on sale about which no one appeared to know anything. The rarest porcelain plates from the great services cost only about a pound or two a piece; Imperial Easter eggs with exquisitely painted decoration of the highest quality were to be had for a few shillings. Glass objects and papier mâché pieces of considerable vintage were at prices which today seem utterly ridiculous, as was sculpture, silver, pictures, books and engravings. One of the most interesting items that came my way was a porcelain snuff box called a *packat-tabatièrka,* an example of the exclusive invention and production of Dmitri Vinogradov, the mid-eighteenth century discoverer of Russia's true porcelain. (I purchased it for five pounds the rate of exchange at the time was $7 to the £1).

At that time in London anything of quality coming from the Soviet Union was considered to have been imported into Russia in the first place. The fact that an Academy of Arts had existed, that the Imperial, Gardner, Popov and the other great porcelain factories had once produced artifacts of levels of excellence similar to Sèvres and Meissen, that glassmaking and enameling had been practiced in Russia since pre-Christian times (pre-988), was the object of disbelief. And nothing was known of the great schools of icon painting—of Novgorod, Vladimir-Suzdal, Pskov, Moscow, the Stroganov and others. Indeed, I was often asked whether Russia was, or ever had been, a Christian country.

Because of the writings and exhibitions of the Wartsky Gallery's chairman, Kenneth Snowman, and a few others on the continent of Europe and the Americas, knowledge already existed of Carl Fabergé's production and of enamels. The work of certain decorative and design artists was also known, due predominently, as has been said, to Diaghilev and the Mir Iskusstva (the World of Art) movement: Larionov, Goncharova, Kandinsky and Malevich, Bakst and Benois, Golovin and Bilibin. But who had ever heard of Rublev and Dionissi, of Borovikovsky and Levitsky, or of the later Repin and Serov?

When I first entered London's art world, much that came from Russia was to me a novelty in those early days. But, my original shop in a quiet London backwater created a mild sensation—and, thankfully, it prospered—more than that, the interest was awesome.

I moved my shop to larger and grander premises in the St. James's area of London where it became a gallery, and all my stock, totally Russian. Shortly thereafter other shops and galleries took an interest and brought Russian art into their agendas. Auction rooms came to me for the identification of various articles until, finally, they brought Russian "experts" onto their staffs. It was all extremely stimulating and encouraging, as well as being great fun.

The only enigma was and continues to be that museums of art have all but ignored the existence of Russian art forms. A recent survey of institutions in the United Kingdom shows that this is still the case in the last decade of the twentieth century. There exists one museum with a collection, however, called Hillwood, in Washington, D.C., that was inaugurated by the late Mrs. Marjorie Merryweather-Post. Her interest in Russian art forms was stimulated when she lived in Moscow as the wife of Joseph E. Davies, the United States ambassador to the Soviet government. The Russian treasures that are to be seen at Hillwood are awe-inspiring. They include the well known portrait of Catherine the Great's friend, the courageous Princess Dashkova, painted by arguably Russia's greatest portraitist, Dmitri Levitsky. The painting was once the property of the author's late father, who saw to it that this work of national importance received a worthy resting place.

There are very few locations, therefore, other than the museums of the Soviet Union where Russian art may be viewed and studied in any diversity or profusion. Several collections of some importance exist in the West, but being privately owned they are not accessible to the general public. As a final resort, it is in the auction rooms and the commercial galleries of the Western world where these beguiling objects may be seen and handled. An occasional plate from the service which Catherine the Great gave to her lover, Gregory Orlov; a cup and saucer from the coronation service of Nicholas I; a teapot with the dramataic black eagles from the Gatchina Service, part of which accompanied Nicholas and Alexandra on their final tragic journey. History whispers its secrets to us through these fragments from the past.

CHAPTER ONE

The Russian Icon

*T*he collecting of icons is perhaps the most problematic of all such activities because, in addition to the abundance of fakes, dating can be difficult, especially when heavy restoration has taken place. Before the creation of icons can be discussed, a few words should be said about their development.

When the Great Prince of Kievan Rus, St. Vladimir Ravnoapostolny ("the Equal of Apostles," a title given to those who Christianize a country), entered into a political union with his powerful neighbor the Byzantine Empire, he adopted the Greek denomination of the Christian faith as his country's official religion. The date for this tremendous decision was 988. Mass baptisms in the Dnieper took place accompanied by a certain amount of wailing from the populace when their wooden idols of Peroun of the Silver Head and the Golden Mustache, among others, were thrown to their doom into the river with great ceremony.

The coming of Christianity to ancient Rus was accompanied by a great influx of adjuncts to the faith. Dogmatists and priests arrived from Greece

in order to instruct and to baptize the people, and with them came
engineers and architects, mosaicists and painters of icons.

As the "new" religion spread through the land, many churches and
monasteries were built, all of which needed decoration. The preferred
artistic methods of the time were with frescoes and mosaics. These were
all, naturally, religious in nature, and they were all fashioned according to
strict canon laid down by the senior clergy of the Mother Church.

In Russian the word *ikona* (icon) means "likeness," and in the Orthodox
Christian world of Eastern Europe it is applied to religious depictions
exclusively. The icon originated in the Fayum mortuary portraits of
ancient Egypt which were usually painted in tempera, or by encaustic
techniques, onto well-seasoned and prepared wooden panels. This style of
pictorial art found its way to Greece during the early centuries of the
Christian era. At the same time the Islamic and Jewish abhorrence for
pictorial depiction of the human form also transfered itself to the Byzantine Empire where it was accepted, but only in part. A sort of compromise
was reached and pictorial art assumed a two-dimensional stance with the
third dimension being totally ignored. The third dimension produces
perspective and schematic depth thereby inducing sculptural effects, and
since sculpture in connection with Orthodox religious art was considered
to be idol worship it was, thereby, heretical. This distinction extended to
secular portrait sculpture in the round, which was prohibited in Russia
until the eighteenth century. Religious sculpture is still frowned upon by
fundamentalists today.

The icon was a textbook for the illiterate mass of the people, so absolute
conformity to the Greek canonic teaching was a dicipline to which icon
painters adhered unquestioningly, especially in medieval times. Any individual interpretation of Church dogma or artistic liberty in religious
depiction spelt extreme danger for the presentation of the historical truth
which was the basis of Orthodox icon painting, hence all deviation,
however devotionally sincere, was forbidden fruit.

Despite the Tartar Mongol occupation of the greater area of inhabited
Russia, schools of iconography developed, but only as the country de-

veloped—in different regions and at different times. By the thirteenth century, however, these became identifiable; the fourteenth and fifteenth centuries were the apogee of Russian iconic art. It is generally agreed that the greatest school of them all was that of Novgorod. Novgorodian art always remained clear and distinct from that of the other schools: in its inherent stolidity it was less romanticized than that of central Russia. Colors remain vivid to this day and they contain a certain luminosity; they were used with courage and without fear in juxtapositioning. The Novgorodian artists enjoyed a great deal of stark, white highlighting. The whole produced a combination of profoundly convincing iconography of monumental stature. ·

Other important schools were those of the northern regions where easel painting predominated because most of the churches were built of wood. The icons of Pskov, which is known colloquially as "great Novgorod's younger brother," are also easily recognizable: the work is somewhat austere, a dark-bluish-green is favored, and there is a quaint predilection for pearl ornamentation in lieu of assist (gold ornamentation) on the Virgin's *maphorion* (veil), for example. The delicate elegance of Suzdalian icons contrasts dramatically with those of Pskov. On the final demise of Novgorod's greatness in the sixteenth century, it was Moscow that came to replace the entire spectrum as the cultural center of Russia. The previous greatness of the city had not been so much in its iconography as in the individual artists who had worked there, outstanding men such as Prokhor of Gorodetz, Rublev, Theophanes (or Feophan Grek as the Russians called him as the Spaniards called Theotocopulos, El Greco), Daniil Chorny, Dionissi and other predominently unknown great icon painters of Russia.

Sixteenth-century Moscow contained two major iconographic centers: the Tsars' Armory Palace workshops and those of a family called Stroganov. The latter had been Novgorodian merchants, but when that city incurred Ivan IV's wrath for the independent, indeed republican, stance it had adopted, they removed themselves together with their serfs, artists, servants, goods and chattels to a property in the extreme north called Solvichegodsk. In due course their business interests brought them to Moscow where they established art workshops and began to produce icons of superlative grace and delicacy, which finally earned for them the unprecedented distinction of being known as a school of icon painting in their own right. The Stroganovs also produced enamels of high quality, a fact which is not widely known.

As time progressed and Western influence became ever more pronounced in all spheres of the country's life, realism began to menace the purity of Russian iconic depiction. The spiritual dimension of the icon grew ever more obscure, and the austere, stylized Mothers of God became beautiful, Italianate madonnas.

During the reign of the second Romanov Tsar, Alexis, an artist of distinction began to work at the Armory Palace art workshops. He commenced his career as a draftsman designing fortifications, working on cartography, and preparing designs for gold and silver objects for the Imperial household and the State. After the recognition of his talent by the Armory's director, the Boyarin Hitravo, his work assignment was changed to include iconography, in which medium he made his name. He was Simon Ushakov (1626–86).

In the beginning Ushakov worked conventionally and produced work that was excellent but uninspired. Gradually his research into the work of contemporary foreign artists in the Tsar's employ induced him to experiment with realism. He began to combine the old ways with the new, a matter of shadows and of detail, especially around the eyes, and he brought genre into his backgrounds. He wrote the treatise *A Word to the Lover of Icon Painting* in which he stated that, like a mirror, iconography should reflect the world's realism. His work, although it went against all the principles of canonic teaching, was accepted with rapture by the Tsar, his fundamentalist Patriarch Nicon and by the people. Ushakov was elevated to the rank of nobility, a rare occurrence for an artist at that time. His work, however, did not suffer from the adulation, and he came to be known somewhat optimistically as "the Russian Raphael." His work produces controversial discussion to this day. None-the-less it can be said that he was the last great iconographer of Russia.

Fourteen years before the death of Ushakov a son was born to Tsar Alexis, whom they called Peter. By 1689 this child, now a youth of enormous stature and energy, had attained sole tsardom, and Russia began her transition from being a backward, disorderly country to becoming the great new Northern Power. Progress was swift and spectacular, but the greatness of the traditional, stylized icon was doomed, never to return.

From that time on there is very little that can be said regarding iconography. Icons continued to be painted, as they continue to be painted even today. This is not to say that excellent work was not produced, and often in the same manner as earlier styles . Many of those in the oncoming coterie of secular artists (whose work will be discussed in the coming chapter) began and ended their lives as painters of icons, but their production was more of a craft than an art, however beautiful its execution. However, for the Russian people, whatever the style in which an icon was painted, an icon remained an icon, it remained an object for veneration and an intercessional means for communication between man and his Maker. Any discussion concerning artistic content or commercial value was, and in some cases remains, a heresy.

It is necessary for collectors of icons to study the historical backdrop against which they were painted. A selected bibliography at the end of this book provides suggestions for further reading. The more knowledge that is gleaned, and this, of course, is applicable to all collecting, the more certain the identification of an object and the greater the appreciation. In regard to icons, a certain knowledge of their construction is helpful because it affects the collector's ability to date a panel. Frescoes and mosaics, as they are painted in situ, cannot be collected and so will not be discussed here.

Easel-painted panel icons were all constructed in a similar manner from wood that was usually of local growth: lime, pine or sometimes oak.

Because wood is a living thing and is altered by the aging process, slots were cut into the backs of the panels into which cut-to-size, harder wooden pieces were inserted to prevent warping; these are called *prolojhny,* sometimes *shponki.* Before the invention of the woodworking plane, an axe was used to smooth the surfaces of wood. Careful examination of a panel for telltale marks can help with the dating of an icon.

The wood that was used, naturally, had to be well seasoned. After the panel was prepared, it was gessoed (gesso consists of a mixture of glue, chalk and water *(levka)* which was permitted to dry). The gesso was then scored with a knife and a strip of textile was attached. Several additional layers of gesso were applied with each layer being left to dry thoroughly. The panel was then ready for the *znamenshchiki* to incise specific outlines to guide the work of the artist–client. Some artists, naturally, preferred to create their own designs, and to trust for inspiration to guide their hands.

Icons were traditionally painted in tempera (a mixture of color pigments, egg yolk, glue or gum—the sap of a fig tree can be used—and holy water), but oil paints began to be used for some work in the seventeenth century. After application, any gilding on an icon received a final polish with the tooth of a wolf, or when it was available, with the larger one of a Siberian tiger. When the image was finished, a layer of varnish *(oliffa)* was applied, and after it had dried a final polishing was administered with the palm of a hand, or with a fragment of pure silk. The icon was then taken to a church for consecration.

A further detail should be considered when an icon is being examined: its *craquelure.* These are rhythmic crazings which should be studied carefully; if a suspicious break in their confluence is perceived, then restoration has taken place or, indeed, the icon could well be a fake. Total confidence in dating early icons precisely is seldom achieved, and many icons must pass through one's hands before the distinctive characteristics are understood.

In order to make oneself familiar with icons one should view them in profusion, handle them, look at the painting techniques through a strong magnifying glass no matter how good one's eyesight may be. If an icon is dirty, touch a corner of a panel with a moist finger and observe the vividness of the colors that exist beneath the grime; it should also be remembered that grime can be artificially applied. Smell the icon; ancient icons are often imbued with the fragrance of the centuries of incense and smoke from candles to which they have been exposed. If a panel is cracked, it can be repaired by a competent, experienced restorer of icons whose expertise is quite different from that of a picture restorer. (An auction gallery can provide an introduction.) Unless an icon is of exceptionally great age, a crack reduces its commercial value, particularly if the crack extends across a subject's face.

Very often icons which appear in the West have been roughly sawn through, and consist of several sections. This is the result of smuggling, for sections are easier to carry than one large icon. A flourishing industry exists in such activity. African students from the Lamumba and other universities in the Soviet Union, nameless gentlemen from Middle East countries, diplomats and political dissidents among others, including the ill-fated Ararat football team, used to bring such goods to my gallery. If they carried clearance papers from British customs, I and everybody else were free to buy from them. A sixteenth-century icon in my collection was once part of a vast, life-cycle depiction of St. Nicholas gracing a large church or cathedral, and came to me through such a source. The original icon had been sawn into small individual pictures which were battered and scratched. They were exquisitely restored by a talented British artist, and set into individual wooden forms with raised borders (*kavchegs*) painted and crazed to match the *craquelure* on the paintings.

Early Russian icons were never signed by their creators. They were painted to glorify the Almighty, and not for personal conceit. Late in the seventeenth century signatures began to appear on the backs of panels, and by the nineteenth century the fronts of panels were often signed.

It may be of interest to the reader to know that a Russian Orthodox institution exists in New York State at Jordonville. The Holy Trinity Monastery. It incorporates a seminary, a printing shop and an art studio where icons are painted, the monastery itself and a cathedral. The Holy

Trinity Cathedral contains a good display of frescoes and icons that were painted by the Archimandrite Cyprian and his pupil the Bishop Alypy. The *iconostasis* is a thing of beauty, though not quite traditional since the Tsar Gates are painted with a depiction of the *Znaiminye,* another name for the Virgin of the Sign, the seated Mother of God holding the Child on her lap: "Therefore the Lord Himself shall give you a sign. Behold, a virgin shall conceive a child and shall call Him Emanuel" (Isaiah 7: 14). The icons themselves are painted in a typical nineteenth century style, an ancient style that is infused with a good deal of realism, particularly in the *liki* (faces of the Holy Ones). Visitors are welcome, and, no doubt, icons may be purchased to aid the monastery's maintenance. Certainly advice and explantions regarding iconography can be obtained there. I should also add that the architecture of the monastery structures such as the cemetery church as well as the cathedral are a delight.

CHAPTER TWO

Russian Pictorial Art (Eighteenth and Nineteenth Centuries)

*T*o collect Russian paintings today is a commendable and highly recommended occupation, and one that should be encouraged. Because very little attention has been given to the country's arts, investments are among the most lucrative. Although excellent work is still available, the market cannot remain in the present state for much longer. Indeed, judging by the prices that are now being realized at auctions, Russian art has already been "discovered" by the West, but not sufficiently as yet to preclude a really good buy for a price that is not nearly as high as it should be. This does not apply, however, to the work of the avant-gardists. (They will be discussed in the chapter entitled Heroic Communism.)

The story of secular painting in Russia is a fascinating one because prior to the seventeenth century it did not exist. The preceding chapter introduced the reader to the evolution of the icon, its flowering and its decline, though only as an art form which transferred its brilliance to a new style of visual art, namely, to realistic, secular pictorial depiction. The connecting link was *parsuna* painting.

The term *parsuna* is a corruption of the Italian word *persona* which describes the style in which the initial, tentative steps were taken by Russian artists to transfer their work from stiff and stylized iconic depiction to that of the West's realistic, fluid and unrestricted presentation. It was exclusively to portraiture that the transition was made. The early portraits were sometimes painted on icon panels, as was the well known depiction of Prince Skopin-Shuisky (a political activist and military commander during the Troubled Times, the *inter-regnum* of 1605-13). Across the top of this panel, the prince's name is written in complicated Church-Slavonic script, as was the custom. *Parsuna* portraits seldom appear on the West's commercial markets, as they are rare, and may be seen only in Soviet museums. But paintings with the *parsuna* element in them are often encountered because the tendency lasted well into the eighteenth century.

As has been said, Peter the Great brought numerous highly paid specialists, technicians and professors from the West to help him introduce Western knowledge to his people. During the process of building the much-needed port on the Baltic—his Window on the West—St. Petersburg (Leningrad today), he closed the Moscow Armory Palace art workshops and transferred them to his new capital city. The icon painters and artists he installed in the Printing House, an adjunct of his Office of Works, to which he attached some foreign artists to instruct the Russians in the West's technical language.

Many of the foreign men who came to work in Russia were artists of established prominence in their own countries; such a one was Louis Caravacque. He arrived in St. Petersburg in the company of eminent architect J.B.A. Le Blond in 1716, and lived there until his death in 1754. He painted portraits of the Tsar and his family, and later of the two Annas, the Empress and the Regent. His greatest contribution to his adopted country was his total devotion to his students and his introduction of them to topographical composition. He was among those foreigners who established an artel.

True iconography died. The school of Russian painting was born, first the portraitest, and later in that century to include other subject matter. Artists, attracted though they were to experiment with novel approaches to depiction, found great difficulty in ridding themselves of the traditional, time-honored habit of painting directly onto a given surface without mixing colors on a palette, of infilling contours with flat coloring and using shadows as dictated by canonic stricture. But the old style was eradicated and soon a new generation of Russians came to rival their foreign masters in the excellence of paintings produced.

Among the earliest to emerge from Tsar Peter's "nest of fledglings" (as he called his young artists) were three men of considerable talent: Andrei Matveiev (1701-39), and the two Nikitin brothers, Roman and Ivan (the former's exact dates are not known, the latter's are 1690-1740). All three men were brought to the Printing House from the Moscow Armory Palace. Despite his short life, Matveiev achieved a certain renown. His double portrait of himself and his wife, although unfinished, underlines this talent. The work is authoritative and pleasing. It is interesting that near the end of his short life he reverted to iconography and painted for the cathedral at the fortress of Saints Peter and Paul which was being constructed at that time under the direction of the Swiss architect Domenico Trezzini.

The Nikitins' work was prolific. Of the two, it was Ivan who was the better known artist, and possibly the greater one. He painted a number of portraits of the Tsar and various members of his family, as well as of the nobility. He was best known for his mortuary portrait of Peter, but he left it unsigned and today it has been tentatively attributed to Danhaur. His association with the Tsar led him to paint a stirring topographical rendering of *The Battle of Kulikovo Field,* which is considered to have been the first picture of such a scene in Russian secular art.

Ivan Vishnikov, a competent artist in his own right, was among the first

Russians to act as tutor at the Printing House. His reward came when the Empress Elizabeth commissioned him to paint her portrait, for which she paid two hundred rubles. Elements of *parsuna* stiffness are often visible in his work.

Among Vishniakov's pupils were several men who achieved standing and recognition for their work, but of whom very little is known in Western Europe. One such man was Alexi Pavlovich Antropov (1716-95), whose lifespan covered most of the eighteenth century. He painted all the Tsars and Tsaritzas, as well as the more celebrated people of the time, including the Kings Teimouraz and Irakli of Georgia. Early in life he had traveled extensively through the Ukraine and investigated industries, particularly textile production, where he admired the glorious colors and patterns which are later visible in the garments of his future subjects. He also became fascinated with *finift* (the painting of miniatures on enamel), and experimented in such work extensively. He is reputed to have painted many *Dame à Portrait* insignia badges for ladies of the Court, but these are unsigned so it is not known which of the ones that remain are his creations. These are very collectable, but also very expensive items for they are always set in diamond frames.

Towards the end of his life when his eyesight had begun to fail, he was appointed by the Holy Synod (Peter the Great had abolished the Patriarchate) to investigate the well being of icon painting in Russia, in particular the Stroganov School in Moscow. In his will he left his house in perpetuity, as a dwelling place for young artists, many of whom had been his pupils. Among them was Dmitri Levitsky, the greatest portraitist Russia has ever produced and a man of international standing.

The Printing House of Peter the Great was often mistakenly called the Academy of Arts, but that august body's inauguration did not come about until the reign of Elizabeth, on November 17, 1757. Serious Russian pictorial art can be calculated from that date. In fact it was only from that time that painting came to be recognized as a medium of fine art in its own right in Russia, and received a place of its own on the Academy's agenda. Up until then it had been only architects, engravers and sculptors who were considered the true artists, and inevitably a state of disgruntled resentment prevailed. But, as the Academy's initial French directors strove to establish the curricula, rules and standards, which were necessary to mold the Academy of Arts into a body worthy of its name, a new factor developed to cause bad feelings between the foreign and domestic artists. Native artists simply could not find work because the foreign ones—the very men who had taught them—were extolled and lionized by fashionable society, and were given entry into the most exclusive circles where commissions were available, the doors of which were closed to the Russians. These matters were finally resolved but a certain resentment remained, even in Soviet literature to this day.

Among the first instructors at the Academy of Arts was Anton Pavlovich Lossenko (1737-73), a Ukranian, who was an artist of great talent and creativity in his own right. He was among the first men in Russia to study the painting of daily life, a subject of which the Academy disapproved—it had already formed a preference for work executed from the imagination, preferably based on mythological allegory. Lossenko's *In the Artist's Studio* is among the earliest of Russian genre paintings, which came to be known as "classes of home function."★

By the accession of Catherine II (the Great, 1762–1796) a school of Russian painting was already established. The era was dominated by a triumvirate of truly great artists. Fedor Rokotov (1735–1810) was trained under le Lorrain and Pietro Rotari (creator of *The Gallery of Graces* at Peterhof which is now called Petrodvoretz). Vladimir Borovikovsky (1757–1825) was a *fin de siècle* style, Westernized icon painter who developed into a portraitist of tremendous stature; his best known work is, perhaps, a portrait of the Empress Catherine walking a whippet in her

---

★*In the Painter's Studio* has now been tentatively attributed to another artist, but one of less renown, Ivan Firsov. A signature was uncovered during the painting's first cleaning. However, since early Russian painters very often followed in the iconographer's tradition and did not sign their pictures, attributions and reattributions are a common feature in the identification of paintings. Firsov's signature could well have been a fake. Lossenko very seldom signed his pictures.

park. The third man was Dmitri Levitsky (1735–1822), mentioned earlier, who painted *The Empress Catherine as Legislatrix* and *The Smolianki,* a magnificent portrait of the architect Kokorinov. Posthumously Levitsky came to be known as "the Russian Gainsborough"—the crux of the matter is that Gainsborough was never called "the English Levitsky," for Russian artists had barely been heard of at that time. All three men lived on into the nineteenth century, a century which was as dramatically innovative for Russian art as the eighteenth century had been.

There are many artists of the Russian eighteenth century whose names would be included here if space allowed. Their work often appeared on the commercial markets of the West in recent decades for nominal prices. No one seemed to know whom the portraits depicted, or indeed, whether they were of Russian origin or not. Today their value has risen a hundred-fold and more.

The very early years of the nineteenth century in Russia were devastating because of Napoleon's rampages which culminated in his invasion of the country in 1812. All habitation along the route of the Grande Armée, as well as Moscow, was vandalized. Restoration was the order of the day once Napoleon had been vanquished, and there was little time for art. War artists such as Ivan Terebeniev (1775–1864), whose cartoons of the wars appear occasionally on the markets of the West today, had had their moments of glory, but a new spirit prevailed in the land.

The entry of Alexander I (1802–25) into Paris in 1814, and subsequent occupation of it in concert with his allies, brought him and his officers into close contact with neo-Classicism. Although it had existed in Russia for some years, that of France nevertheless created a great impression on the Russians. With the final cessation of hostilities a fashion for it rekindled dormant embers, and continued to flourish in every sphere of the Russian arts. By the 1830s, however, it was dead as it was in the rest of Europe, and tastes in general went into decline. Russian pictorial artists remained strong nonetheless, and an impressive coterie of new painters came to the fore.

Gradually Classicism gave way to Romanticism in art, the first intimation being in the work of a young artist, Oreste Kiprensky (1782–1836). A product of the Academy of Arts, in 1805 he won its gold medal for a work called *The Battle of Kulikovo Field.* The award carried with it a stipend for foreign travel, which he did not avail himself of until 1816.

Kiprensky was predominantly a portraitist, and executed his pictures in the manner of the time with uninspired backgrounds and great concentration on the faces and hands. As his work was recognized as outstanding in quality, commissions for it increased: his predominant output was paintings of the *beau monde,* the milieu in which his great talent had brought him to move. He painted the Emperor, his remarkably beautiful wife as Psyche, the writers Pushkin and Zhukovsky (also an artist) and various other notables. When life as a fashionable portrait painter began to irk, he took himself off to Italy where he remained until 1823. A scandal in connection with an artists' model brought him hurrying home, but a good deal of Italy's sun and warmth remained in his brush and his work became lighter and more colorful. He was flattered and feted, but his popularity waned when some periodicals accused him of producing *tableau de genre* of a private, *gnilovo* (putrid, rotten) nature—Kiprensky often painted erotica. His nature restless, his temper short, he returned to Italy in 1827 where he became a Roman Catholic, married his murdered model's daughter, Marousha, and painted pictures simply to make a living. They were banal and eclectic and not of the standard of which he was capable. He died in Rome unmourned and unsung other than by his loyal wife. Posthumously he came to be known as "the Russian Ingres."

There were many contemporaries of Kiprensky whose work brought Russian standards up to those of Western Europe. One such was Karl Bryulov who, although he is considered by many to have been the most powerful and dynamic artist of his day, nevertheless produced work that more or less was of the same quality as the *oeuvres* of Kiprensky and the younger Alexandre Ivanov. He was the son of an Italian named Briollo before Russification: it is also said that his father was a German woodcarver at the Academy (the anomalies in research bring art historians unending headaches). Like both Kiprensky and Ivanov, he was a product of the Academy, and like them he won its gold meal which provided him with foreign travel. In 1822 he left for Italy in the company of his brother Alexander, whose destiny was to become one of Russia's greater architects, and remained there painting for nineteen years.

Bryulov is best known for his masterpiece, *The Last Days of Pompeii,* which he painted in 1833; it brought him international renown. After a certain amount of travel he finally returned to Russia on the crest of the proverbial wave, where he immediately opened an attack on the Academy of Arts, accusing it of despotism, a lack of imagination and restrictive practices. He was horrified by its unrelenting and didactic stance forbidding artists to deviate from stricture, to paint, in Russian parlance, "from the soul." It was he who prevailed upon the later artists, Perov, Purikov and Kramskoy, to continue the fight for liberation from the Academy's short-sightedness. A prolific artist, Bruyulov left 708 (known) canvases to posterity.

Alexandre Ivanov (1805–58) was temperamentally Bryulov's opposite; he was quiet and retiring by nature, and when a gold medal from the Academy took him to Italy, he remained there for twenty-seven years of self-imposed exile. He painted several pictures of considerable importance during those years, including studies of nude figures set against Italian landscapes (e.g., *Youths on the Shore of the Bay of Naples*) in which the bodies glow in the sunlight with an ethereal luminosity; the pictures are replete with *plein air* and can be said to be forerunners of Impressionism. But it was not until his return to Russia that mysticism and religion took hold of his imagination, and he began to concentrate upon religious depiction, though not on iconography.

It took Ivanov an unbelievable twenty years to prepare and complete his masterpiece, the renowned *Christ's Appearance to the People.* The painting failed to please the public at its first showing, which broke the artist's heart. It underwent criticism from every quarter, including Alexandre Herzen in far off London. The reason why it did not altogether please the general public was because such subjects, until recent times, had been reserved for iconography exclusively, and possibly the populace were chary of accepting such a blatantly secular approach to a sacred subject. Nineteenth-century Russia was a deeply devout country, and iconic subject matter was regarded as being beyond any form of artistic expression. Even the magnificent individual pictures of Christ that were being painted by various artists—by Kramskoy, Gay and others—were met with a certain embarrassed reservation.

Ivanov died at the early age of fifty-two of cholera. A few hours following his death a *skorohod* (a palace messenger) arrived to say that *Christ's Appearance to the People* had been bought by Nicholas I for inclusion in the State Collection.

An artist whose stature remains as great as those of the afore-mentioned was Alexei Gavriilovich Venetzianov (1780–1847), but his style differed from the others so greatly that no comparisons are possible. The blending of Romanticism with Realism is particularly pronounced in the work of this one-time pupil of Borovikovsky. His painting is often compared to that of Jean Baptiste Greuze for its gentle colors and fluidity of movement. But Venetzianov was a romantic, both pictorially and spiritually. He romanticized his subjects to an extent that was, at times, incongruous, but with a sincerity that precluded criticism.

Venetzianov entered the Academy in 1810; in 1812 his talent procured for him the title of Academician. He never traveled, but went on to work as a land surveyor, and when he had accumulated sufficient money he purchased a modest estate in the government (country) of Tver called Safonovka, where he established a school for artists—peasant lads, anyone who appeared to have a flair for painting was accepted, whether he could pay for his tuition or not. Some seventy pupils passed through it in the course of his twenty years of running the school.

Venetzianov never neglected his own work as a painter and is best known for portraits of peasants set again vast and majestic landscapes—he caught the poetry of Russia. Possibly his best known picture is the *Barn,* which is not an exterior, but a well composed symphony of light and shade playing upon a group of men and women at work within an architectural interior. It was bought by Nicholas I for the State Collection, and the 5,000 rubles that he paid for it helped Venetzianov with improvements at his school for artists.

Venetzianov appears to have been a very nice man and he was generally liked, but, for some reason, not by his fellow artists. He met his end in 1847 when he was thrown from his sleigh on an icy road. His paintings are found occasionally on the Western markets: one delightful picture of a peasant woman nursing her infant beside a bush in an open field appeared in a small London auction room. It was described as a portrait of an Austrian peasant. The general bidding stopped at £28.

An artist called Pavel Andreievich Fedotov (1815–53) was a man whose life ran concurrently with that of Venetziannov, but his vision of the world was totally different, and his work was, more often than not, critical, satirical, sometimes caustic. His early years were spent in the army so he never received technical instruction but like the earlier Mikhail Shybanov, his hand was guided by a natural talent. A bitter, disillusioned man, niceties did not worry him over much, yet he was capable of producing such pictures as *Vdovoushka (The Young Widow),* in which the woman stands leaning against a bureau on which a portrait of her late husband reposes next to an icon of Christ, while she appears to be packing. The picture is imbued with an exceptionally compassionate understanding of life.

That of Fedotov was a puzzling personality, and sadly, an unbalanced one. He voiced his problems in his pictures. In his more rational moments, however, Fedotov was capable of producing incisive portrayals of the Russian national character, in much the same way the Englishman William Hogarth did of his countrymen.

Fedotov's choice of subjects for ridicule and satire broke with accepted contemporary tradition, and brought his work to the notice of the authorities. Yet he avoided serious trouble because his talent protected him, as it did the poet Pushkin in some of his more radical work. Fedotov was a rebel at heart, and his approach to painting was a forerunner to that of many of the Wanderers, members of a movement that came into being some ten years after his death.

Emperor Alexander I's devotion to the pictorial arts was minimal, but portraiture was his one weakness. He admired and promoted the work of the English artist George Dawe (1781–1829), a Royal Academician, and gave him space at the Winter Palace in which to establish a studio the Emperor often visited. Dawe's series of paintings showing the monarch wearing the uniforms of different regiments, as well as the 1812 gallery of portraits of the participating officers, are the best known of the Englishman's work.

The first half of the nineteenth century transported Russia from an era when portraiture alone represented the country's pictorial arts into one which genre entered the backgrounds, and when land and waterscape painting finally found approval from the Academy of Arts. A short summary follows of the more prominent artists' names who have not been discussed here.

I. AIVAZOVSKY (1817–1900), the greatest Russian land- and waterscapist—best known for his renderings of the Black Sea.

F.A. BRUNI (1800–75), best known for the *Bronze Serpent at St. Isaac's Cathedral in Leningrad*.

K.D. Flavitsky (1830–66), a pupil of Bruni; best known for his rendering of Princess Tarakanova, who is said to have been the illigitimate daughter of the Empress Elizabeth and Razumovsky.

M. IVANOV (1748–1823), landscapist and watercolorist; attached to Prince Potemkin of Tauride on military campaigns as Official Artist; painted oil portrait of Potemkin in civilian dress.

A.E. KOTZEBU (1815–89), son of writer and illustrated many books; Court painter.

L.F. LAGARIO (b. 1827), friend of Aivazovsky; seascapist. A. E. MARTYNOV (1768–1826), one of Russia's first waterscapist.

A.O. ORLOVSKY (1777–1832), born in Russia but Poles claim him as their own; lithographer and water colorist; delightful, imaginative artist, specialized in portraying Cossacks, Bashkirs and Kirghizes.

S.S. SHCHUKIN (1758–1828), pupil of Levitsky; painted portraits of Paul I and the Empress Maria Fedorovna.

M. SHYBANOV (dates not known), serf on Potemkin property, painted five portraits, among these, *Catherine II in Traveling Dress.*

P.I. SOKOLOV (1753–91), pupil of Levitsky; allegorical and mythological subjects.

V.A. TROPININ (1776–1857), serf; pupil of Shchukin; portraitist; painted *Pushkin, Mmme. Shchepkina, A Guitar Player.*

G.I. UGRIOUMOV (1764–95), pupil of Levistky; painted topographical battle scenes; rector of Academy of Arts.

A. N. VORONIKHIN (1760–1814), portraitist and architect.

M.N. VOROBIEV (1787–1855), pupil of Thoma de Thomon; portraitist, later landscapist; assistant to Alexeiev on exploratory expeditions into Siberia in 1809.

M.A. ZITCHI (d. 1905), historical and genre painter; some portraits.

Among the greater foreign artists who lived and worked in Russia, many of whom made the country their home were : J.B. Leprince (1734–1781), Count P. Rotari, Stefano Torelli, L. Tocqué, J.B. Lampi, Marie Antoinette's friend Madame Vigée Lebrun, J.L. Deveilly, Charles G. Geissler, the de Groot brothers, van Loo, Christineck and Caravaque, George Dawe and John Augustus Atkinson (nephew of the famous engraver), J. Walker, Delabarthe, Damame-Demartrai, Fory-Mayer and numerous others.

CHAPTER THREE

Russian Pictorial Art (Nineteenth and Twentieth Centuries)

*I*n 1825, having put the Decembrist Revolt down with an iron fist, Tsar Nicholas I ascended the throne of all the Russias. He inherited a nation that had had a full century to assimilate Peter the Great's reforms, to consolidate all that he had attained on Russia's behalf, and to expand artistic endeavor in every conceivable direction. He also inherited bad relations with Persia, whose attack on Russian possessions in Transcaucasia resulted in the war of 1826–28. The year 1828 saw war against Turkey in connection with Balkan problems, which were resolved in 1829, alongside the first stirrings of the Pan Slav movement in opposition to the Turks' treatment of subjugated Orthodox peoples.

An era of official championship of Orthodoxy, autocracy and nationalism dawned, largely in reply to the beginnings of Russian socialism, guided from abroad by a renegade, illegitimate nobleman, Alexandre Herzen (1812–70) and Mikhail Bakunin (1814–49). Two decades later (1853–56) was the Crimean War, during the course of which Nicholas died and his son Alexander II (the Tsar Liberator, responsible for the Serf Emancipation Edict of 1861) replaced him on the throne.★

Such was the scenario against which the Russian artists wrought their miracles.

During the middle years of the nineteenth century the Academy of Arts had continued ponderously and laboriously on its obstinate way. It was, of course, an extremely necessary institution for it maintained discipline, produced professors of the highest caliber for its students' tuition, provided the possibility for cultural tourism and a certain amount of tuition abroad and organized large exhibitions, but it also stipulated total conformation to its various editcs. It was the continued preference for painting from the imagination as against nature and its disapproval of experiments and innovation of any kind that finally led to serious divisions in the country's artistic structure. The problem began in 1863 with a students' revolt: thirteen of them, and one sculptor, refused to sit for their examinations, their excuse being that a free choice of theme had been

---

★The Russian serf system was introduced during the reign of Ivan IV (the Terrible) in order to tie the peasants to the land on which they lived because a great exodus into the northern and southern regions began when certain new conscription laws displeased the people.

Russian serfdom was not the same as the American slave system, and there were no slave markets. Technically, a serf belonged to the land all of which belonged to the Crown, so a peasant could not be bought or sold. Abuse of this system certainly took place, as exemplified in Tolstoy's *War and Peace* when Count Rostov purchases a particularly splendid cook.

In 1803 new legislation permitted a peasant to purchase his and his family's freedom, and a landlord to grant it. Total emancipation came in 1861, at which time a peasant became liable for taxation and conscription. Prior to this a landowner was responsible for all such matters on the peasants' behalf.

In the U.S. formal emancipation was instituted on January 1, 1863.

denied them. They were voicing a latent protest against artistic strictures, and the revolt was not a political one.

An artist called Vasilli Perov (1834–82) was a prime mover in all these matters. He was a man of meager means, son of an impoverished nobleman, and he had worked hard at the Academy in order to ensure a traveling scholarship. Upon receiving the award in 1862 he departed for Paris. The year of the students' revolt found him there, but he was not happy or content. This was a time when French art was passing through a period of troubles: the *Salon des Refusés* had taken place and public opinion was in a turmoil. Gustave Courbet (1819–77) was fighting his own Academy as Perov was destined to fight his. In England, artists had formed the Hogarth Society in opposition to their Academy of Arts. In '64 Perov returned to Russia where, being in sympathy with the students, he joined their leaders, Kramskoy (1837–87) and Purikov (1832–90, a professor at the Academy), and participated in the controversies. In time, however, Purikov found the protestations too extreme and returned to the Academy's justly agitated bosom.

The French Realist painters among whom Perov had lived and worked left their imprint on his thinking, and his better known genre paintings reflect this. *The Country Sermon, The Easter Procession Through a Village* and *The Police Inspector* all contain a hearty social criticism of events. Their content earned them censorship by the state, but the directive was later rescinded, and they remain anecdotal, somewhat jaundiced, yet resoundingly interesting records of that era. Indeed, this description may be applied to most of Perov's work. Like Terebeniev and Fedotov, Perov was his own man, and he refused to be swayed by political pressures and the accompanying insidious literature that endeavored to sway artists into anti-establishment pictorial depiction. Since illiteracy was rampant, the picture, like the icon of yore, still acted as the textbook of the mass of the people.

As an artist, Perov's work was meticulous, his drawing true, his detail scrupulous, his colors, initially a trifle muted, later lively. This strange metamorphosis took place at the time when he was commissioned to paint pictures of historical interest—*The Pugachev Rebellion,* for example. A series of portraits of contemporary notables painted for the merchant-prince Pavel Tretiakov were less colorful, but highly competent.

Perov's friend Nicholai Kramskoy was an artist of similar ability, but concentrated almost exclusively on portrait painting. His rendering of *An Old Man* is not unlike Nicholas Gay's (or Gé) *Self Portrait.* They are both symphonies of dramatic *chiaroscuro* with white hair and heavily lined faces set against starkly black grounds. Gay was the greater artist, but Kramskoy's contribution to his country's world of art was the spirit he contributed to the student movement and genesis of the *Peredvijhniki,* the perambulating artists, or the Wanderers as they came to be known in the West.

At the time of the students' revolt, it was the Academy which had been the adjudicator of the direction art should take. Afterwards it was the Wanderers, and they prospered amid a state of general euphoria when most of the leading artists of the day joined their movement. Regrettably the three decades during which they were operational were marked by a certain deterioration in the quality of production; once the disciplined influence of the Academy was abandoned and with it the possibility for cultural travel, tutorial standards went into a decline and reflected in workmanship. The Academy itself, of course, continued on its way and remained a respected, if somewhat static, institution. The spirit of adventuresome experiment upon which the Academy frowned, together with the newly found freedom of expression, however, stirred many artists of the day to ever more diversified production. But a general tendency toward mirrorlike painting remained in most Russian work throughout the epoch.

Writers and political activists such as Chernishevsky, author of *Aesthetic Relations of Art and Realism* (1855), were vociferous in upholding the Wanderers and in inciting them to engage in political contentions by imbuing their work with material of social (preferably anti-establishment) significance. Chernishevsky contended that it was an artist's duty to expose injustice, poverty, social inequalities—his main interest was not *how* a picture was painted, but *why*. His writing, in fact, produced an outburst of protest from Tolstoy, Griboiedov and Turgeniev, and from the Rector of the University of Moscow, Pletnev. Some artists agreed with his theories, others did not, but Chernishevsky pre-empted Socialist Realism by some seventy years.

The Russian Revival occurred in the second half of the nineteenth century, with a revival of general interest in Russia's turbulent but colorful heritage. Books were written on the subject and folio volumes were sponsored by the government called *Antiquities of the Russian Empire*. The historian Dmitri Rovinsky (1825–95) wrote extensively about icons and pictorial art, and he produced seven volumes on the subject of the *lubok* (woodcut) of which he possessed an extraordinary collection. Additional books began to appear on the market by such scholars as N.P. Kondakov, N.P. Likhachev and others of similar caliber. The artist Igor Grabar, published his first volume of a complete *History of Russian Art* in 1909; there were seven volumes planned, but one remains missing, its production interrupted by the Revolution. Today this work is reportedly being translated into English by Soviet authorities.

During the Revival many scholars researched and worked on the history and development of Russian art, its architecture, ancient patterns and calligraphy (the architect Petr Stassov's son, Vladimir, wrote a tome about the latter), dress and fashions. A pseudomedieval art form evolved which came to be known as the Russian style, the greatest exponents of which were the artists Vasnetzov and Vroubel, Bilibin, Kustodiev and Korovin and certain others whose work will be discussed shortly. Paintings of rousing patriotic and national subjects also created great interest and enthusiasm. Nicholas Gay was an enthusiastic supporter of this style even though he was a markedly academic painter himself.

In 1857 Gay won the Academy's gold medal which sent him roving through Europe, where he came to rest in Florence and remained for twelve years. In 1869 he returned to Russia and joined the Academy's staff as a professor. The delightful landscapes that he had painted in Italy were forgotten and he turned to painting huge canvases of historic and religious subject matter, but not icons. Today many of these paintings are termed national monuments. In time Gay grew dissatisfied with his life and retired to his estate in southern Russia where he concentrated on farming. A friendship developed between him and Lev Tolstoy, whom he drew and painted many times, and it was the latter who persuaded him to return to St. Petersburg and to his former role in the country's arts. Upon the death of Kramskoy in 1887, Gay found himself elected to head the Wanderers, but he did not remain in this post for long, for his character was morose and he was not a leader of men.

Among the better known pictures that Gay painted are *Peter the Great with His Son, Alexis, Catherine the Great at the Tomb of Elizabeth;* two years before his death he painted a terrifying *Crucifixion* and a still more disturbing *Golgotha.* Gay sometimes painted with blood which, hopefully, was not human! His rendering of *Christ at the Mount of Olives* is a monumental study of a man's pent-up emotions, with a seated, thoughtful Christ set against an interplay of light and shade cast by the surrounding trees. His understanding of schematic depth and perspective are wonderful, as is the strength and magnetism of his artistry. A further noteworthy characteristic of this artist's work is the extraordinary truth of expression on his subjects' faces. Gay's portraiture, at times, is on a level with that of the eighteenth-century master Dmitri Levitsky.

A career which ran parallel with those of Kramskoy, Perov, Gay and Tolstoy was that of Vassili Vereshchagin (1842–1904), who was a convinced pacifist and evangelized his convictions in his work. Accepted tradition depicted glory in the victory of battle, but he painted its agony and cruel slaughter. The impact of his pictures was immediate as was his international acclaim. He worked as Official Artist in the Russo-Turkish War of 1877, and painted three detailed canvases of its resulting horrors in addition to many sketches and drawings. Between the years 1888 and 1903 he painted a good deal from imagination, and produced a series of shocking spectacles of Napoleon's invasion of 1812. These pictures pleased Tolstoy sufficiently to include them as illustrations of *War and Peace.* Vereshchagin was appointed Official War Artist during the Russo-Japanese

War of 1904–1905. He went down with the battleship *Petropavlovsk,* when she went out to meet the Japanese Grand Fleet that had bottled up the Russians at Port Arthur. War, his arch enemy, claimed its illustrious prize.

Another artist who painted rousing scenes of historical interest was Vladimir Surikov (1846–1916). He was born in Siberia and most of his early pictures were of that locality and of religious subjects, but not icons. He was disposed to painting pictures of vast dimensions and in a range of colors that probably influenced later artists in their choices. In 1881 he moved to central Russia and joined the Wanderers. His better known work includes a near Impressionistic *Suvorov Crossing the Alps* and the well-known *Boyarynia Morozova* (an Old Believer zealot). The detail and psychological insight into each individual character in the drama are truly remarkable. *The Execution by Peter the Great of the Rebellious Streltzy, The Conquest of Siberia, Yermak* (a sixteenth-century Cossack explorer), and others all brought him renown. In addition to his competence and great talent, Surikov's strength lay in his ability to project the atmosphere of an era. Surikov is considered to have been one of Russia's giants in the arts, as was Isaac Levitan.

Levitan (1861–1900) is known as the poet-painter of Russia, for he was imbued with an exceptional love of beauty in nature, which he painted with authority, sometimes with austerity, with a minimum of brushstrokes and no strong accents upon central features. His communion with nature was such that he would weep openly on beholding some quiet rural scene that touched his heart. He seldom strayed far from Moscow where he lived. He was adopted by Stanislavsky's Alexeiev Circle, and was prevailed upon to create the scenery and costumes for Chekhov's play *Chaika (the Seagull),* first produced in 1888. Levitan succumbed at a young age to tuberculosis, but his work lives on in the museums of both Eastern and Western Europe, and the Americas.

The only artist who came close to equaling Levitan's stature as a landscapist was Mikhail Nesterov (1862–1942), who was a pupil of Serov. He also painted many subjects connected with the church and with prayer. He joined the *Mik Iskusstva,* a movement that was in the process of replacing the Wanderers, but found the ambiance too worldly, so he left them. He painted a series of psychologically penetrating portraits, but finally reverted to religious and mystical preoccupations. Nesterov executed some decorative work at the Catherdral of St. Vladimir, at Kiev, and in several other churches. The overall experience that is conveyed when examining Nesterov's work is of great calm; his landscapes are never agitated but fuse unobtrusively into backgrounds, and a certain sadness invariably encompasses the whole. *The Vision of St. Bartholomew* illustrates them perfectly. The only fault that can be ascribed to this artist's work is a weakness in the depiction of the human face.

Nesterov did not leave Russia with the coming of the 1917 Revolution, but continued to work, predominently on portraits. The fact that he won numerous awards for his work—he was a State Prize-winner in 1941 and Honoured Artist in 1942—indicates that this one weakness had righted itself.

There are two additional men whose names should be included here: Repin and Serov. The former (1844–1930) was born in Chugaiev where he worked in a provincial iconic workshop under a man called Bunakov. He then moved to St. Petersburg in 1863 and entered the Academy in 1869, where one of his teachers was Kramskoy, who persuaded him to join the Wanderers.

During an excursion down the Volga, Repin was inspired to paint the river's boatmen in a a portrayal which he called *Burlaki* (the Bargemen), which the world came to know as *The Volga Boatmen*. This painting, characteristic of his strong bent for realism, was a courageous venture in Russia of the seventies for it encapsulated political suggestion—poverty and deprivation—matters that were frowned upon by a nervous censor's office. Yet blind eyes were turned on Repin's painting because it was so clearly overt and uncomplicated, and it was accepted for what it was, a perfect work of art. *Burlaki* took Repin three years to complete, and he did this with tenderness and insight. He depicted a group of men, exhausted, worn out by life, with a bewildered, youthful novice in their midst. They are shown pulling their boat along with all their weight braced against the river's current. The panorama is stark yet not depressing, and it conveys a sense of isolation. The painting was exhibited at Vienna in 1873, where it brought the artist immediate success and acclaim. It was later purchased by the historian, the Grand Duke Vladimir Alexandrovich (maternal grandfather of Princess Marina, the late Duchess of Kent, England), who acquired a magnificent collection of this artist's work.

Paradoxically, Repin was appointed to a professorship at the Academy of Arts in spite of being a member of the Wanderers, and he remained with both organizations all his life. The artist/historian Igor Grabar considered that it was a certain indecisiveness, together with a total lack of ambition, that precluded Repin from becoming a figure of world stature, for his talent was immense.

Among Repin's better known works, in addition to *Burlaki,* are *The Return of the Unexpected One, Ivan the Terrible after the Murder of His Son* (which is considered to have been his greatest work), *Zaparojhtzy* (*A Letter to the Turks from the Zaparojhtzy Cossacks*) and *The Tsarevna Sophia* (Regent during Peter I's and Ivan V's cotsardom). He also painted many portraits and made innumerable sketches and finished drawings of his contemporaries—in pencil, charcoal, sepia, gouache—Moussorgsky, Borodin, Tolstoy, Eleanora Duse, the architects Stassov and Ton, and of some of his fellow artists including one of Serov whose talent rivaled his own. Both Repin's and Serov's work represent a magnificent record of the epoch and its social history. During the Revolution of 1917, Repin emigrated to Finland where he lived with his daughter Vera, and continued to paint. At that time he reverted to a great extent to painting icons. He was a devout man, so in the sad circumstances of exile, this is understandable. Having lost the country that he loved, Repin died of a broken heart on September 29, 1930, aged eighty-six.

In 1865, Valentin Serov was born in Moscow, the son of the eminent musician Alexandre. At the age of nine he became Repin's pupil, and in 1888 was accepted by the Academy for tuition. In 1894 he joined the Wanderers, but five years later he left them to join the *Mir Iskusstva*. Five years after that he resigned from the Academy.

Serov was a political animal and his sympathies were with the left, yet paradoxically he painted a series of superb portraits of the Imperial family, of Alexander III and of his brother the Grand Duke Pavel Alexandrovich, as well as two delightful depictions of Nicholas II. In spite of his politics and his presumptuous quarrels with the Empress, he always remained on excellent terms with the Emperor. He also painted many of his contemporaries, including particularly interesting studies of his father, of Repin, of the Princesses Zinaida Youssoupova and Olga Orlova, and of the impressario Mamantov's daughter which he called *A Girl in Sunshine*.

According to the artist/historian George Loucomsky, Serov's portraiture contained so much brilliance that "he pierced the insides of men with the mercilessness of a Dostoievsky." It was, indeed, his portraiture that was his strength, but Serov never parted from his pencil. His laconic, essentially linear drawing, his virtuosity in portrait sketching, like Repin's, reached sublime heights. He was often unkind to his sitters, and as in the work of his predecessors, Fedotov and Perov, his work often contained barely concealed satire, political suggestion and vitriol. There was no vitriol, however, in his numerous portraits of his theatrical friends, of Karsavina, Duse, Korovin and Chaliapin, Diaghilev and Ida Rubinstein among others. A poster which he produced of Anna Pavlova for her appearance in Diaghilev's 1909 presentation of the Imperial Russian Ballet in Paris shows her *sur les pointes* and wearing the long tutu of the day which appears to have consisted of moonbeams. Another of his endeavors that contains no satire is a series of illustrations for some of Krylov's fables, with each animal's characteristics lovingly and intelligently expressed, and exquisitely executed.

Whether consciously or not, Serov imbued his work with a good deal of the Impressionists' style, dispensing with the preparatory sketch; but their typical broken line was not for him. His use of color varied. It was sometimes bright and pure, at other times muted and gentle as in the manner of the Salon artists, and his work was replete with *plein air.* Serov died in 1911 thus escaping the heartbreak of World War I and the horrors of 1917.

There are still many artists who could be discussed, but the more important ones have been included, and an indication has been given of the progress that was made in the pictorial arts in pre-revolutionary Russia. All these artists' work can, of course, be seen in the museums of the Soviet Union, but other ways are open for the persistent enthusiast to come to know these painters and their pictures.

First, ascertain the dates of forth-coming sales of Russian art in auction rooms, and then attend the previews. The catalogs contain an outline of each picture or artifact, sometimes with considerable detail, written by auction house experts.

Secondly, investigate commercial galleries which handle such things and, as stated earlier in this book, pay the gallery regular visits.

Thirdly, read and research.

CHAPTER FOUR

The Mir Iskusstva

*T*he years preceding the formation of the *Mir Iskusstva* (the World of Art, similar in many ways to the French Nabis group,) in 1886–1887 were characterized by exploratory probes, as they were when the Wanderers had formed their ranks to breath new life into the Russian arts. When the Wanderers' impetus began to wane, the Mir Iskusstva was there to match them in interest, as in time it was itself matched by the avant-gardists.

The turn of the century, saw a great deal of movement in the arts of Russia, and conventional genre and realism lost ground to the various branches of non-figurative art. Ideological currents deflected any hope of a comprehensive direction, yet they were recognized by international historians and critics as being interesting and exciting directions in themselves.

Very little was known in *fin de siècle* Russia about the innovations that had been taking place in French painting since the mid-nineteenth century. The Impressionist manner of applying paint in small touches of pure color and painting in conditions of *plein air* caused their work to appear dazzlingly bright, as well as less restrictive and complex than that of the Salon artists. All this was new to the Russians, but neo-Impressionism with its various branches came to be accepted and assimilated so that an entire new work–force emerged to produce work of the very highest caliber. Other than its superb colors, the more extreme of the avant-gardists' work cannot be said to have been understood and appreciated by the greater proportion of the people—particularly by the peasants.

The immediate forerunners of the avant-garde and of the designer artists, whose work dominated the initial years of the present century in Russia, were men, and the few women who had begun their incursion into the arts, but not yet formed loyalties to one or the other of the two media. One such man was Victor Mikhailovich Vasnetzov (1848–1927). His style of work was that of the Slavic Revival or *Rouskii Stil*.

Vasnetzov was the son of a priest who studied for a while at a seminary. The Church's disciplines, however, were not for him and he entered the Academy of Arts instead. In 1876 he went to Paris, where his lightweight scenes of café life were of small importance and showed no hint of the great talent that lay dormant within him. He returned to Russia the following year, and it was at this time that his fascination for folklore came to life. Like Grabar, Bilibin, Korovin, Maliavin and many artists of that generation, Vasnetzov became totally Slavic in his tastes and began to research into medieval Russia. His rendering of the legend of the Tsarevich Ivan and the Grey Wolf (Ivan has just rescued a maiden and they are escaping on the back of a delightfully fluffy wolf) is as well known to Russians as the story of *Uncle Tom's Cabin* and *Peter Pan* are to the West.

Vasnetzov also painted historical pictures such as *The Baptism of St. Vladimir* and *The Aftermath of Prince Igor's Battle with the Polovtzy*. His excursions into conventional genre are exemplified by *The Threshing Floor*. He seldom painted icons, although he worked for a while on the frescoes at the Vladimirsk Cathedral at Kiev which, for him, were a singular departure. His best known work is possibly *The Bogatyri* (three Russian heroic knights).

At the request of Savo Mamantov, founder of the Mamantov Theatre in Moscow which rivaled Stanislavsky's Moscow Arts Theatre, Vasnetzov made his debut as a theatrical designer by creating the scenes for Ostrovsky's play *Sniagourochka* (the *Snow Maiden*) and in 1886 for the *Snow Tsaritza*.★ It was a characteristic of this era that many of the country's leading artists designed for the theater. Mamantov was the first to use established artists to design for his production; until then inexperienced and untalented artisans had been employed to design for his productions. Vasnetzov's strength lay in his imaginative composition and use of color, which was why his work for Mamantov proved so successful.

Mikhail Alexandrovich Vrubel (1856–1910) was a neo-Impressionist *par excellence,* though the Symbolists claimed him as their own. He was a man of great sensitivity, with an approach to religious depiction reminiscent of the icon painters of old. He was an unhappy man with a mental instability that tortured him, and which eventually brought about his total insanity; he lived out his last five years in an asylum. When he was commissioned to restore some important frescoes in the church of St. Kiril at Kiev, he recognized the extent of the compliment that had been accorded someone of his youth and inexperience. Very little was known at that time about the restoration of icons and usually only experienced artists were used for the work. His work at the Kirilovsk church awoke in him a keen interest in Byzantine frescoes and mosaics, so he travelled. He studied Veneto-Cretan icon painting which he preferred to that of Greece, and investigated the work of the great Italian masters in Venice. He remained there for a year, and when his money ran out in 1885 he returned to Russia. But memories are short, and he found that he had been forgotten in his homeland. His fortunes waned and he suffered extreme poverty.

Vrubel lived from hand to mouth, but there were times when lucrative commissions came his way, and they provided him with the breathing spaces he needed to work upon the things that interested him the most: the techniques of water color absorbed his thinking for a long time. Russian mythology also fascinated him, as did the language of color and the

---

The word *Tsaritza* is sometimes incorrectly rendered *Tsarina*, but there is no such word in the Russian language. *Tsarevna* is a medieval term for a Russian Tsar's daughter, the word *Tsarevich*, a Russian Tsar's eldest son. In 1712, Peter the Great changed the title Tsar to that of Emperor.

various means of its application. All served to spur him on in enterprise. Vrubel was a man of erudition but small drive, a not unusual combination. It was only when Mamantov finally located him and brought him to Abramzevo that he was able to work, and to give his talent free rein once again.* He came alive only for a short time.

Vrubel's everlasting search for style, form and idiom produced a great variety in his work, discernable in such paintings as his decidedly Slavic *Pan,* some portraits of unknown women, and in the various narrative depictions of an ethnic character including his well-known *Bogatyr* (1898) (the latter depicts a larger-than-life medieval knight who is seated on a larger-than-life horse), and in his various renderings of *The Demon.***

The Demon tells the story of the Fallen Angel's infatuation for a mortal Georgian girl, the Princess Tamara, and the despair, revengeful rage and accompanying emotions he experiences when she rejects him. The poem by Lermontov which tells the story of the Demon was transformed into an opera by Rimsky Korsakov's pupil, Anton Rubinstein; it is an opera which, sadly, is never heard in the West. Vrubel painted this subject many times, possibly identifying the Demon's anguished soul with his own.

Vrubel's life is frequently compared with that of Paul Cézanne (1839–1906), for neither man received true recognition during his lifetime. It was only at Abramzevo that Vrubel received a peace of mind and an opportunity to work with no pressures to disturb his concentration. Like Cézanne, he also painted still life, some icons for the chapel that stood near the house and some stage designs for the Mamantov Theatre. Had it not been for Mamantov's intervention in his affairs and his practical help— there were no government subsidies and little private patronage for the

---

*Abramzevo, close to Moscow, once belonged to the writer Sergei Aksakov, and was acquired by Mamantov in 1870. It became a center of importance for every category of artist, and many lived and worked there. It rivaled Stanislavsky's Alexeiev Circle, which was supported by millionaire Moscow merchant Savvo Morozov.

**Vrubel's version of the Demon's fateful encounter with Tamara was very often reproduced by the Lukoutin and Vishniakov factories onto papier mâché boxes and other objects. The work of the earlier artist Venetzianov was also a favored subject for reproduction.

arts—the world would have been deprived of this sad man's *oeuvres* and the avant-garde artists of the inspiration with which he fired them.

Another artist of the period whose work can be described as fantastic on occasion, yet which was totally different from that of both Vasnetzov and Vrubel, was Ivan Bilibin. He was born on August 4, 1876, into the well-to-do St. Petersburg family of a Surgeon Rear Admiral of the Russian navy. He was enrolled in the Law Faculty of the University there and in 1825 was provided with an introduction into the art world when he entered the School for the Advancement of the Arts. He completed both establishments' curricula with credit and departed on an extended tour of western Europe in 1898.

On his return to Russia in the autumn of that year he entered the art school at Talashkino that was run by Princess Tenesheva (a personal friend and a loyal and active supporter of Diaghilev and the Mir Iskusstva). It was there that Bilibin met the great national master Ilya Repin and was invited to attend his lectures at the Academy of Arts. In 1899 Léon Bakst introduced him to Diaghilev.

In addition to his general artistic competency, Bilibin's forté was his wondrous imagination, which channeled his ideas in a consistent and logical development. His work enriched the world with glorious color (usually flat plains and basic colors) and delightful visual images of refreshing novelty. The Mir Iskusstva played no small role in his development, and through the society's publication his work made contact with the West. It was from European Russia that he drew his inspiration. He researched his country's legends, folklore, children's tales, paintings, architecture, epic heroes and saints—he entered into Russia's very soul. In 1899 he began to illustrate fairy tales. These were presented to the public at the Mir Iskusstva's second exhibition in 1900, where many new young artist's work first saw the light of day. ★

★The Mir Iskusstva society mounted many exhibitions in St. Petersburg, but it did not take them on tour as did the Wanderers.

Bilibin found himself drawn ever more strongly to book illustration, and commissions for his graphics came streaming in. His illustrations of books and poems brought him national recognition. V.M. Maximov and M.V. Dobujhinsky were his only rivals, though neither man was as prolific as he.

He worked in a markedly Russian style, which was paralleled in the West by the neo-Gothic, and his art exuded nostalgic, though not cloying, charm as well as an innate intelligence. His illustrations included *The Little White Duck, The Feather of the Finest Falcon, The Firebird, Babba Igga and Koshchei the Deathless One, The Frog Princess,* Pushkin's tale of *Tsar Saltan* (set to music by Rimsky Korsakov), *Grad Kitez, The Choosy Bride, Boris Gudonov* and many other texts.

In the early 1900s his talent was sought by Diaghilev and other impressarios for work on theater and costume designs, an occupation at which he came to excel. In the years 1908 and 1909 Diaghilev took the opera and ballet companies to Paris, and Bilibin was one of the designers for some of the productions that astounded Western Europe. He went from one achievement to another, but with the Revolution he moved away from Russia. By 1925 he and his family had reached Paris where he worked primarily for Diaghilev. Finally, for reasons best known to himself, in 1936 he returned to Russia and left his family in France. On arrival in Leningrad he was swept up into that city's artistic lifestream. His final work is said to have been water color depictions of *Bogatyri* (epic heroes), but these have not been seen in the West. Bilibin died in February of 1942 in the horrific siege of Leningrad.

Theatrical design was a medium that was new to most artists at that time, but they adapted, and many came to work for the Mamantov and Moscow Arts theaters, and also for Diaghilev, who helped most of them to their feet. Diaghilev was a man of extraordinary energy and vision, and his favorite role was that of guide, mentor and father figure, a role in which he excelled. His particular strength lay in an uncanny ability to discover talent. He watched over every aspect of the arts, bringing them together to form the remarkable synthesis which earned his productions international fame and acclaim. With the demise of the Mir Iskusstva publication in 1904, the aesthetic essence of the Wanderers also finally ceased to be an influence on Russian artistic life.

The many references to the Mir Iskusstva in the preceding pages substantiate its immense influence on the turn of the century Russian arts.

Its founder-member was a young artist and art critic named Alexandre Benois, who was a Russified Frenchman whose family had made Russia its home since the eighteenth century. He and his close childhood friend K.A. Somov (1869–1930, son of Hermitage Museum Director, a genre painter, portratist and illustrator) were both products of the Academy of Arts. Among their friends they listed Dmitri Philasophov, a writer, and Walter Nouvel, whose interest lay in music. Upon conclusion of their studies the four frequently met for lofty intellectual discussions. It was the time when avant-gardists were being investigated as was Art Nouveau. Others joined them and jocularly they became known as the Nevsky Pickwickians, but the group soon decided to take their name from their common interest which was, of course, world art. Hence, The World of Art, or Mir Iskusstva. They retained this name for as long as the movement lasted.

In the mid 1890s Philasophov introduced his cousin whom he called Seriojha to the group. Seriojha, in fact, was Sergei Pavlovich Diaghilev, who was tolerated by the others for his cousin's sake, although his appearance and general behavior was that of a dandified fop, and intellectually he was the least cultured of them all. Little did they dream that he was the man who was destined to bring all their wildest hopes and aspirations to fruition. In due course Diaghilev's driving ambition formed the Mir Iskusstva into a serious and coherent society for the promotion of Russian arts. One of Diaghilev's major talents was an ability to deal with people, and it was he and not Benois who became the nucleus of the society's activities.

Gradually most of the remaining Wanderers came to join the Mir Iskusstva until the list of members read like the *Russian National Biography of Art*. All that was needed was a publication to promote their theories, and to bring Western art to the Russian public's attention. A young French diplomat Charles Birlé joined the group if only for one year, but he proved to be an invaluable asset. He introduced members to the French Impressionists and to many writers on the subject, Baudelaire, Verlaine, Huysmans, and to Richard Müther's *History of Nineteenth Century Painting*. The society was then well armed with material for a publication (of the same name). The first issue was printed October of 1898, and the Mir Iskusstva's first exhibition took place in the same year.

The vehicle for a new direction had been provided for the arts, for painting, for ballet and the opera, though not so much for the dramatic stage, and a fashion was set for the revival of neo-Classicism, especially for its furniture. Diaghilev and the Mir Iskusstva revived a national interest in the eighteenth-century protraitists; Diaghilev wrote an excellent biography of Dmitri Levitsky. Financial contributions continued with unexpected generosity: the Emperor gave ten thousand rubles a year, and continued to do so until the outbreak of hostilities against Japan in 1904. At which time the publication of the journal stopped. It had served its purpose, and its originators moved on to other things, predominently the theater. The Mir Iskusstva movement, however, continued on into the 1920s and in exile.

Having divested himself of the responsibilities of his magazine's production, Diaghilev threw himself into a new venture to bring Russian art to the West (see Introduction). He was in Paris when the Revolution struck and never saw his homeland again.

Running parallel to Diaghilev, the Mir Iskusstva and the artists who surrounded them, as well as the traditional painters who continued in their particular neo-Academic styles of work (V.D. Polienov, I.I. Shishkin, B.M. Kustodiev, S.A. Sorin, L. Pasternak), yet another movement had been developing in Russia: the avant-garde. The pre-revolutionary avant-garde was limited to a comparatively small coterie of artists, some of whom played a dual role in maintaining contact with, and often working in, the more conventional world of the Mir Iskusstva style. Goncharova was in this category.

Nathalia Sergeievna Goncharova (1881–1962) was a descendant of the poet Alexandre Pushkin, and like him was not only a Slavophil, but a pronounced Russophil. She studied at the Moscow School of Painting, Sculpture and Architecture where her tutor was the prominent sculptor Prince Pavel Troubetskoy. She received a silver medal for her sculpting, but very quickly turned to painting. "Sculpture," she told Jean Merechal of *Le Petit Parisien* in 1937, "cannot convey the emotion produced by a landscape, the moving fragility of flowers, the softness of a sky in spring. I renounced it because I was fascinated by the play of light, the harmonies of colour." (*Goncharova,* Mary Chamot, page 8.) In about 1900 Goncharova met Mikhail "Misha" Larionov, and an association began which was to transform both their lives.

Very few women had been active in the Russian pictorial arts before the end of the nineteenth century, and Goncharova was among the first to receive recognition. An exhibition mounted by the *Zolotoye Runo* (the Golden Fleece) group finally established her and Larionov as the undisputed leaders of the more progressive avant-gardists of the day. Goncharova was a most versatile artist, although Cubism, Symbolism, Constructivism were not for her, she experimented with them all; she always said that the discipline of Cubism was her inspiration. She delighted in neo-Impressionism, which is evident in her paintings of flowers, trees, certain landscapes, yet an element of the *parsuna* style which must have been derived from her love for icons is very often discernable in her work, hence her participation with Larionov in Primitivism. She also experimented with *Luchism* or Rayonism, based on the concept that the crossing of reflected rays of light created spacial forms, which resulted in such delightful pictures as *Cats* (1911–12) and *The Green and Yellow Forest* (1912). The former may be viewed today at New York's Guggenheim Museum, as can Larionov's *Glass*.

Goncharova's association with Diaghilev began in Russia where she worked on some of his productions, and this later continued in Paris. In 1915, in response to a summons to join him at Lausanne, she did so. A meeting was being held there to discuss the production of a new ballet which they named *Liturgie*. Lydia Sokolova agreed to dance the role of the Virgin Mary and Léonide Massine that of the Angel Gabriel. This ballet, however, was never produced because Stravinsky, considering it to be sacrilegious, refused to compose the music for it.

They all moved to Paris, Goncharova having been joined by Larionov. In France they both continued to paint, he free-lance on private commissions, she predominently for Diaghilev's various productions, but their days as trend setters were over. Still, some magnificent work was later produced, such as *Le Coq d'or* designs. She had worked on the 1909 and the 1914 productions, but it was for the Paris production of 1926 that she surpassed herself; the curtain that she painted for it brought her international acclaim.

In 1955 Goncharova finally married Larionov (1881–1964), an artist of dynamism, innovation and tremendous imagination which was often bawdy and erotic. He participated in exhibitions that were given by the various avant-garde groups, those of *The Light Blue Rose, The Yellow Jacket, The Donkey's Tail* and *The Jack of Diamonds,* sometimes, though less often, with those of the Mir Iskusstva. He sometimes mounted his own shows even during his years of National Service. He published his *Rayonist Manifesto* in 1913, an experiment considered to have been the foundation for abstract art in Russia. He seldom worked for the theater, but concentrated on his own uninhibited, boisterous production. He was able to join Goncharova at Lausanne in 1915 because a wound received during the Tannenberg action had provided him with a discharge from the army.★

★Larionov's main ambition was to create an essentially Russian style and to move Russian art away from the extraneous influences of the French Impressionists and the German Expressionists.

The man who was the most dramatic and the busiest of the post-revolutionary group of exiled painters working for Diaghilev was Lev Rosenberg, known as Léon Bakst (1868–1924). In Russia he had been at the Academy, from which he was expelled for painting pictures in derision of icons. He became a portraitist, and his work came to the attention of the Grand Duke Vladimir (brother of Alexander III), who was an enthusiastic patron of the arts and author of considerable knowledge and authority. He became the young artist's benefactor and opened many doors. In due course Bakst met Benois, Philasophov, and finally Diaghilev, and he joined their group. His first commission was to design for a ballet called *La Coeur de la Marquise* for the Mariinsky Theatre, and in the same year for *La Fée de Poupées*. He went on to work on decors of four productions: *Narcisse, l'Après-Midi d'un Faune, Hélène de Sparte* and *Daphnis et Chloé*. Other than his several years as a fashionable artist and portraitist, and unlike Goncharova, Larionov, Malevich, Kandinsky ,and others, he was never a part of the experimental world, and his life was dedicated almost exclusively to the theater.

Bakst's first serious opportunity came when Diaghilev commissioned him to design for *Cléopâtre,* which was one of the ballets presented in Paris in 1909. In 1910 *Shéhérazade* was presented in Paris with Bakst's designs producing a sensation, against which Karsvina's and Nijinsky's performances rose to unprecedented heights. In addition to the intense essential vitality in his art, there appeared to be a hypnotic element in the admixture of Bakst's range of colors, an element that suited theatrical production to perfection.

With civil war raging in his homeland, Bakst found himself in Paris once again, this time on a permanent basis but still working for Diaghilev. He collaborated with him on *La Belle au Bois Dormant* in 1921, which is considered to be among the most difficult ballets for which to design; on *Sadko* and *Phédre,* both in 1923, as well as many others of innovation and brilliance. The brilliance, despite their constant quarrels, had led Diaghilev to employ him more often than any of his other designers, which

invoked bitterness towards him in many quarters. A lonely man, Bakst
died in 1924 in the *banilieu* of Paris. He left few friends to mourn his
passing, but a legacy of work which few artists ever succeeded in equaling.

A man, however, whose work did equal Bakst's, but in a totally
different manner, was Alexandre Benois, a *force majeur* in his country's
arts. Diaghilev, himself, seldom made a serious decision without first
consulting him, even if he did not always agree with his conclusions. As
an artist, Benois' style was gentle, fluid, elegant and imaginative; he
designed for many of Diaghilev's productions—his particular favorite
being *Le Pavillon d'Armide*—he was the first artist chosen to design for it
(1907).

Benois' contributions to the various areas of Russia's world of art appear
to have been limitless; he was able to look back upon a great many
achievements during his years of exile in France following the Revolution.
He had mounted the most spectacular exhibitions in addition to those of
the Mir Iskusstva, including one at which ancient icons were presented as
an art form for a first time in Russia, with the work of the greatest ancient
masters on display. He had designed for both the Mamantov and the
Moscow Arts Theatres, for numerous operas and ballets. His costumes
and scenery for *Petroushka* in 1913, for which Stravinsky composed the
music, were possibly his most outstanding work.

Like most neo-Academicians, Benois was wary of the "ists," and together with Diaghilev, he was careful in selecting those who were permitted to contribute to the Mir Iskusstva's exhibitions and publications, of
which he was the editor. Goncharova and Larionov were *persona grata* in
his circle, as was Kandinsky. Benois was also wary of the Symbolist
publications, *The Scales* and *The New Way,* because, although they carried
a good deal of his own magazine's thinking, the more extreme of the
avant-garde artists were beyond his (willing) comprehension, indeed appreciation. To many of them, of course, his own work was decidedly
vieux jeu.

In his exile Benois continued to design for the Paris Opéra and others which sought his services. He lived out the remainder of his life in Paris in the care of his daughter Attia. He died there in 1960.

Among those artists who left Russia in the revolutionary years were Roerikh and Pasternak, Sorin and Somov, Loucomsky and Dobujhinsky, Alexandre Yakovleff *(Le Croisière Noire)*, Golovin, Seribrekova and Stelletsky, the Pevsner brothers (Gabo) and Chagall.

The *oeuvre* of Mark Chagall (1889–1985) is unique. He was born at Vitebsk on the river Dvina into a large (seven brothers and two sisters), close family of Orthodox Jews with whom he lived until 1907, at which time he departed for St. Petersburg to study art and to seek his fortune. In 1910 he went to France to continue his studies, for he delighted in Matisse and hoped to meet him. He read his *Notes d'un Paintre* (1908) avidly, and this Impressionist's theory that free and spontaneous brushwork liberated an artist's instinct influenced him always. Chagall painted everything, floating lovers and violins, clowns and cats, chandeliers suspended from stormy skies, Madonnas and crucifixions, winged creatures, roses and candles, extraordinary birds on the lines of Sirin and Alconist, horses and carts leaping out into the skies, and magnificently imposing rabbis, *The Rabbi with a Lemon* being one of the more delightful ones. His dynamism is exemplified in *Exodus* and *The White Crucifixion. The Cemetery Gates,* painted at the height of his Cubist period (1917), demonstrates the distance he traveled artistically in his later work and subsequent intellectual development.

Chagall strode from one success to another. Even the Revolution left him unmarked, for Anatoly Lunacharsky, Soviet Commissar for Education, elevated him to the post of District Commissar for Fine Arts and Director of the Vitebsk Art School. Chagall did not remain in these posts for long, for among the various problems he encountered were his unending disputes with Kasimir Malavich about the latter's desire to reduce Constructivism to a few geometric basic shapes and forms called Suprematism. These disagreements caused Chagall to move back to Moscow

where a new and exciting post awaited him. He was to create a Jewish
State Theatre and act as cultural designer for it. The site chosen for it was
the Kamerny Theatre. Chagall was delighted with this appointment, and
worked hard to make the theater a success. Gradually, however, he grew
disillusioned with all that was taking place round him: Lenin was insisting
that art be totally concerned with, and concentrated on "Heroic Communism." There was the distinct prospect that Socialist Realism would
become a model for all matters connected with the arts, which caused a
revulsion in Chagall. His illusions were shattered, and he appealed to
Lunacharsky for help in obtaining exit permits for himself and his wife. In
1922 the Chagalls left Russia for Paris, traveling by way of Berlin where
he produced the *Mein Leben* etchings.

Chagall's life was a happy one and both his marriages were a success. In
1930, somewhat prematurely, he published his autobiography *Ma Vie,* but
although many years were to pass before his death, this publication
provided his posterity with a fascinating self portait of the inner man. A
great artist, he died on March 3, 1985.

The work of all the artists discussed here can be found on the markets of
the West, some more easily than others. The more important auction
galleries now hold sales once or twice a year which are exclusively dedicated to Russian pictorial art, and a few galleries are beginning to specialize. Diligent attention to these as well as perusals of specialist books
bring inestimable rewards.

The more important artists who worked during the eighteenth and
nineteenth centuries in Russia have been discussed in these chapters, some
regrettably only briefly. It is hoped that the reader has gained an understanding of the art forms and their creation, and why the seventeenth
century has been all but omitted in the history of Russian pictorial art. The
turn of the seventeenth to eighteenth centuries was a time of confusion in
these arts, which, as shown, rallied very quickly to compete on similar
levels of production as those of other countries. It is interesting to note,

however, that tourists who visit the U.S.S.R. today show infinitely more interest in the work of the icon painters of old, than in any other art form.

Russia may not have had a Michelangelo, Raphael or Tinteretto, but she had the iconographers Rublev and Dionissi, and many other predominently unknown and unrecorded painters whose work was no less formidable.

CHAPTER FIVE

Palekh and Papier Mâché

*T*he history of the village of Palekh bears no relation to the papier mâché industry for which it is renowned today. Palekh came into being during the years of Tartar occupation when the Vladimir-Suzdalians fled from the onslaughts on their cities by the Golden Horde. To protect themselves, some of these people settled on the banks of the Paleshka River in heavily wooded terrain—terrain which the Tartars' mounted armies disliked and generally left in peace—and they named their village Palekh. Among the settlers were monks who were painters of icons. They built a chapel, trained their neighbors in the secrets of their art, and the community grew and prospered. The style of iconography that was practiced by the Palejhians was refined, miniature-like and delicate in depiction, not unlike the product of the latter day Stroganov School of Iconography in Moscow (to which, in fact, they lost many artists, and vice versa). Palekh became one of the leading schools of icon painting in Russia, though not among the greatest.

The village of Palekh, in the district of Vladimir and not far from

Mistra, another icon-painting center, once belonged to the Princes Skaradobsky, but when the family died out the village reverted to State ownership. In the first quarter of the seventeenth century it was presented to a nobleman, Ivan Boutourlin, in reward for services to the State, and it remained in that family's possession until 1861, the year of serf independence. Emancipation, however, made very little difference to the Palejhian artists, the village did not disintegrate and there was no mass movement to other parts of the country as in many other areas of Russia. The industry continued in much the same way as it had done during the preceding centuries.

Palekh made its contribution to iconography when stylistic decadence set in during the seventeenth century; it was able to follow its own path, bypassing to a great extent the Italianate, realistic tendencies of the era. As time went by, however, it also suffered: its style became over-ornate and complicated, and too many figures were crammed onto small panels. The flora and fauna also became increasingly realistic, as did the landscapes and backgrounds, and genre scenes were introduced into compositions. The specialized, abbreviated language of iconography was gradually dispensed with (e.g., *stoupki*★). The *liki* (the faces of the holy personages), however, remained true and stylized, the figures traditionally elongated and graceful, the whole image flat and two dimensional.

Sadly, today Palekh's industry has forsaken the icon and concentrates on papier mâché production which, despite its admitted beauty, cannot match that of its former treasures. Whatever expertise the present day workmasters possess is all due to the industry's inherited past.

The manufacture of papier mâché objects in Russia took on serious proportions when a Moscow merchant called Pavel Korobov set up a small factory in the village of Fedoskino in 1795, and the initial output consisted mainly of lacquered visors for the army. Experiment with manufacturing techniques very quickly brought a wider variety of objects

---

★*Stoupki* are the small excrescencies painted into backgrounds to indicate a mountainous terrain on icons.

to the range of production, and the year 1804 saw 13,000 articles produced. Taper holders, Easter eggs, blotters and trays, cardcases, plaques, and boxes of every kind—snuff, jewelry, glove—were major items of production. In 1818, Korobov's son-in-law Petr Lukoutin took over the business and changed the name from Fedoskino to his own. By 1821 production ran to some 48,000 articles a year.

Success always promotes emulation and other factories came into being, but none could match the sustained quality of the Lukoutin enterprise. Some of the work at the Vishniakov factory, however, rivaled the best of Lukoutin's, but in general the work and the decoration were inferior.

Although the first work of both Fedoskino and Lukoutin is said to have been based on that of the earlier Stobwasser papier mâché production in Germany, trial and error brought the Russians success. Whether in the end the production at one or the other factory was the finer remains a moot point. Suffice it to say that the Russians arrived at their own formula, and it was one which produced excellent results.

The perfected Russian method, in brief, for the production of papier mâché entailed the gluing together of sheets of cardboard over forms. These were soaked in linseed or vegetable oils, then heated. Stiff, water-repellent shells were thus achieved. The papier mâché was removed from the forms, and lids and bases were fitted as required. The resulting objects were painted in tempera, often after grounds of gilding had been applied. The result was a warm glow which shone through the layers of paint and the final lacquering. The painting techniques were much the same as those of icon painters, and as in the final process of an icon, the polishing of the gilding on papier mâché was done with the tooth of a young wolf, or, when available, with the larger one of a Siberian tiger.

Traditionally the Russian boxes were black with red interiors: sometimes these interiors were painted to simulate wood or tortoise shell. The pictures with which the boxes and other items were decorated were usually scenes taken from everyday life of the people, or illustrations from the immensely rich national folk lore: copies of paintings by Venetzianov and scenes from Lermontov's poem *The Demon* were favored. Peasants drinking tea around a samovar, dancers, young lovers trysting, the Kremlin, dashing winter troikas (with sleighs), and summer troikas (with carts or carriages), as well as scenes from Russian mythology and operas were used, but strangely seldom scenes from ballets. Domestic and foreign demand for these goods grew and the industry prospered. The fine gold scrolls that decorate the sides of today's beautiful Palejhian objects were not employed on the earlier production of these wares; neither were the early objects ever signed as they are today.

Both Lukoutin and Vishniakov were awarded prizes at exhibitions which gave them the right to mark their objects with stamps commemorating their distinction. In 1828 the Lukoutin firm was presented with the Imperial Warrant which meant that it then stamped its wares with a tiny golden eagle of State. On the latter day items Lukoutin wares were marked with four additional seals which represented the four reigns during which the firm had been operational. In 1904 the last member of the Lukoutin family died, and due to the outbreak of hostilities against Japan and other financial pressures, the factory closed.

Many of the Lukoutin work force found employment in other industries; some became icon painters, specializing in small *obrazki* (tiny portable icons); others joined jewelers' establishments which demanded fine and delicate workmanship; some moved to the Palekh iconic workshops where miniature work was required. In 1910, however, with the help of the local *Zemski Sabor* (a local council) and a fund instituted by millionaire Moscow industrialist Savvo Morozov, the Lukoutin people regrouped and formed a cooperative known as the Fedoskino Craftsmens' Guild of the Former Artisans of the Lukoutin Factory. Goods marked with this name are fairly often found on Western markets. In that same year (1910) they received a gold medal at the Kazan Exhibition of Arts and Crafts; in 1913 a gold medal was received at a fair at Kiev.

Following the October Revolution in Russia, Palekh's industry forsook the icon, and in the early 1920s turned exclusively to the papier mâché industry. Many of the Lukoutin and Vishiniakov workmasters found their way to Palekh. Together the two groups of skilled artisans rescued an ancient industry from total extinction. In the same way as the seventeenth century Palejhian artists saw the icon through the dangers of total contamination by Western realism, so these men and women saw Palekh's new industry grow and prosper through the days of Stalinist terrors into present times. And the church there that is dedicated to the *Elevation of the Cross,* which was built by Igor Doubov during the years 1762–74, is still lovingly preserved; its magnificent collection of Palejhian icons on the *iconostasis* and elsewhere are a constant reminder of the work that once flourished there when the miniature reigned supreme.

The artists who work in today's Palekh are often descendants of the icon painters of old from whom they inherited their knowledge and technical abilities. They remain the sole guardians of a great and sacred trust.

The icons of Palekh are usually represented by one or two examples at most auction sales where they are clearly identified in catalogs. Their quality, state of preservation and age determines the prices that they attain.

The Lukoutin, Vishniakov and the modern "Palekh ware" goods can be found easily where antiques are sold. If the descriptions that have been given in this chapter are kept in mind, it is a fairly simple matter to establish their provenance. Occasionally, however, boxes and other articles are unmarked. It must then be left to the eye, instinct and knowledge to determine the value of an object.

The prices of papier mâché articles today are difficult to provide. They have risen immeasurably in recent decades, and the markets are fickle entities.

Short Result of Sales lists are provided at the end of this book, giving prices achieved at Sotheby's and Christie's auction houses (London) in 1989–90.

CHAPTER SIX

Adventures in Russian Porcelain

*A*t the end of Europe's seventeenth century, porcelain production was as great a mystery as the philosopher's stone and the elixir of youth. Its secret was jealously guarded behind the impenetrable Great Wall of China where the manufacture of true porcelain was a State secret, and its export brought the Celestial Empire enormous wealth.

In addition to the renowned Silk Road, another existed between Muscovy and Peking along which, twice yearly, treasures and priceless Russian furs and gems were bartered for Chinese porcelains, silks and spices. Peter the Great is known to have possessed a vast porcelain dinner service bearing the Arms of State in his collection. He, himself, had tried to institute porcelain production in Russia, going so far as to employ a man named Eggerbank who claimed to have the secret of its manufacture, but without success. In the reign of his youngest daughter, Elizabeth, a man called Lebratovsky and his assistant Andrei Koursine were hired to explore these Chinese secrets. Their probes, however, also proved unproductive.

None of the eighteenth-century Western European permanent missions in China succeded in acquiring the precious formula either. Many alchemists, who were among the few chemists of the middle ages equipped with any semblance of research laboratories sought the elusive combination. A breakthrough came in Saxony in 1706. The discovery is attributed to a man named Böttger, whose hard-paste porcelain at the Meissen factory caused a sensation, but details of his process are vague because, once the formula had been found, King Augustus the Strong placed as rigid a clamp over it as had the Chinese. It was not until some Meissen workmasters sold their knowledge to Vienna that porcelain was produced there in 1719. The two nations then entered into an agreement to prevent others from gleaning their harvest. But such a course is impracticable, and by various means most European countries soon had their own porcelain manufacturers. This broadly speaking was the picture in Western Europe in the 1750s. Russian, as in most things, followed her own course.

Having failed to penetrate the Bamboo Curtain of the day through her mission to China, Russia endeavored to purchase the formula officially. Several transactions took place involving large sums of money. The Chinese language in which the "formula" was set out, however, proved untranslatable.

In 1742 the Empress Elizabeth ascended the Russian throne. She was a woman of exceptional energy, personality and enterprise, and brought color and sparkle to the somewhat melancholy Court. It was unthinkable that such an Empress should rule without her own porcelain factory since other countries had them! Accordingly, orders went out and funds were made available for its creation.

Because overtures with the Chinese had proved fruitless, it was decided to follow the already proven course, namely of procuring West European craftsmen. A German Konrad Hünger was located in Sweden who claimed to be a friend of the renowned Böttger and to possess the much sought formula. He was duly engaged, brought to St. Petersburg and placed under the direction of an able administrator, Baron Tcherkassov, whose second in command was Ivan Andreievich Shlater.

Tcherkassov's first step was to attach a Russian craftsman to Hunger in order that he learn all that the alleged master could teach. This had become standard practice since Peter the Great's time when large numbers of specialists were engaged at great expense to the Treasury. It was necessary for the imported arts to be absorbed in the shortest possible time because hirelings were not always of the highest moral caliber and were often reluctant to divulge information because they owed no particular loyalty to the Russians. Hünger was such a man. He wasted three precious years pretending to possess knowledge, and produced strings of plausible excuses every time his pretensions were disproved. Tcherkassov finally attached to Hunger the young Russian scientist Dmitri Vinogradov, and it was he who became the creator of the country's first true porcelain (1720–59).★

Upon Hunger's dismissal, the whole weight of the project fell onto Vinogradov's shoulders, with the very serious prospect of the Tsaritza's wrath were his efforts to fail. Although he was to prove his worth, Vinogradov's drinking habits greatly impeded his work, so much so that while he produced noteworthy results, there were periods during which he was chained to his workbench, or, during more violent bouts, he was confined to his room. In spite of these things, Vinogradov did produce true porcelain. Initially this took the form of small cups and saucers, dishes, bowls, jugs, and, most importantly, snuff boxes, for this was an

---

★An intriguing story exists that in early 1747, in a small town called Gzhel which was a prominent center for ceramics, a Moscow merchant called Afanassii Grebenshchikov had discovered porcelain. He opened a small factory, and a local peasant named Pavel Kulikov opened another at Volodino. This porcelain was of inferior quality, but it was porcelain. The story tells that Baron Tcherkassov, for reasons best known to himself, forbade its production, forbade the matter to be discussed and insisted that the formula should be destroyed. The nineteenth century, however, saw porcelain being produced at Gzhel, but although the local clay was of the first order, the porcelain production in that locality was not.

age when a fashion for taking snuff was sweeping Europe. The early pieces were marked on their bases with minute black, sometimes impressed two-headed eagles, the "rivulet" mark or tiny anchors. They are extremely rare and are usually only found in museums, and only in the Soviet Union.

In order to please the Empress, Vinogradov invented the *packet-tabatièrka* which became extremely popular at Court. These boxes were made in various sizes; they were either square or rectangular, always flat, and fashioned to resemble an envelope. The name of the addressee was painted in capital letters on the lid (later a longhand specialist was brought in to help with their production), and it was customary to reproduce the personal crest, or the initials of the "sender" of the envelope, in sealing-wax red on the base.

The earliest information regarding production at the Imperial Porcelain Factory dates from 1751, the year in which Vinogradov produced his first pieces. In 1752 production continued but there was little variety. In 1753, however, production intensified and small articles began to appear in greater numbers. New men were employed, trained and allocated specific areas of work; most of them were serfs from the estates of the Sheremetiev family, and the first of them to arrive was Ivan Chorny. He was very old, however, and did little work of any interest. His son, Andrei, on the other hand, became a skilled and brilliant workmaster under Vinogradov's guidance, and he in his turn trained two gifted pupils: Pimen Troupitzine and Fedor Alexeiev. This was the initial coterie responsible for the creation of one of the most exciting manufactories of European porcelain.

Initially and inevitably Russian porcelain production was guided by the personal tastes of the country's rulers as they followed one another to the throne. Elizabeth's era (1741–62) was one of experiment, trial and error, but eventually items of considerable beauty in design and workmanship had appeared despite her preference for lush and often overwhelming Baroque decoration.

Elizabeth's successor, Peter III, reigned for a few months and left nothing other than his wife's tears to posterity. She succeeded him, however, as Catherine the Great, and the direction that Elizabeth had set for the arts exploded into a banquet of visual delights in her reign. Six new procelain factories came into being (excluding privately owned ones on the estates of the nobility and gentry), among the more important of which was one founded by an Englishman called Gardner.

Francis Gardner arrived in Russia during the second quarter of the eighteenth century. He invested in a property at Verbilki, near Moscow, which he bought from an impoverished branch of the princely Uroussov family. He had purchased some serfs from them at an earlier date, for a foreigner to acquire property with serfs was not permitted. Mr. Gardner appears to have been an astute gentleman! There are many omissions in the story about the beginning of his factory, for it was not until February of 1766 that he received authorization from the Department of Manufactories to operate one. Nor has it been clear until just recently from whom he learned the secrets of porcelain production. It has now been established that he owed his knowledge to another expatriot, a German named Müller.

Johan Gottfried Müller was brought by Tcherkassov from Meissen to work at the Imperial Porcelain Factory shortly after Vinogradov's death (1758). He is listed as a member of the work force on April 25, 1759. In 1763, Müller decided that the entire factory's premises should be rebuilt, and that he should be placed at its head. His demands for remuneration were exorbitant, and the factory was obliged to let him go. It is now established that Müller then met Gardner, and in 1766 was working for the Englishman, and instructing him in the technicalities of porcelain production. Müller was a first class modeler and knew all the secrets of decorating porcelain. It was thus that the great Gardner Factory came into being.

In 1777 a commission arrived from the Empress via the Crown Office for Gardner to design and manufacture a service for sixty persons in honor of the Cavaliers of the Order of St. George, Russia's highest military Order of Chivalry (the receipt of four white enamel crosses constituted a Cavalier). The service was to consist of soup and other plates, tureens, and dishes, bowls and platters, flatware handles, leaf-shaped bowls and baskets with openwork, all decorated with black and orange ribbons and other insignia of the Order. These were to be used for annual dinners given by the monarchs in the St. George's Hall at the great Winter Palace in St. Petersburg for the Knights Companion of the Order.

The commission was obviously filled to Catherine's satisfaction because further commissions for Order services followed: for the Order of St. Andrew the First-Called (Russia's highest non-military decoration) to accommodate thirty persons; for the Order of St. Alexander Nevsky, also for thirty persons. In 1783 the Order of St. Vladimir was inaugurated, and a service for 140 persons was commissioned; a massive service for the Order of St. Stanislav was also produced by Gardner at a later date, and he was presented with the Imperial Warrant for his work.

By command of Nicholas I (1825–55) all order services that had been made during preceding reigns were removed from use and placed on exhibition at the Hermitage Museum (St. Petersburg) and the Imperial Factory was commissioned to make replacement copies of each piece for subsequent use. By command of the same Emperor, the Academy of Arts was urged to investigate and catalogue the country's past achievements in the arts, and *The Antiquities of the Russian Empire* (published in 1852) came into being.

In addition to Gardner, another small factory was founded in Moscow and operated by Carl Milli. In 1811 he sold it to the prosperous Moscow merchant Alexandre Popov, who proved to be an enterprising and talented man for in a remarkably short time he built his new business up to rival his great competitor. By 1817 a census showed some forty-five commercial factories producing porcelain of excellent quality in Russia.

Among the better known factories were the Postygin and the Safronov factories, the Fomin, Batenin, Terekov, the Kisselov-Sapiegin, the Ikonnikov and the Mikloshevsky. The latter factory commenced excellent production in 1836 but lasted only until 1862—towards the end of its existence standards had dropped to lamentable levels due to over-ambitious mass production. Many others suffered a similar fate. Two of the largest were the Kornilov and the Kuznetzov works, but in spite of some excellent pieces their general production also dropped in both the quality of porcelain and its decoration due to the institution of mass production. They survived, however, and extended their enterprises. The vast Kuznetzov combine, after annexing numerous minor factories, finally swallowed Gardner up as well in 1891. The Gardner mark of the later years (St. George in red slaying the dragon set within a circle with the factory's name written in full, the whole surmounted with the Crown of State) was retained.*

The decorative and fine arts of every nation reflect the current tastes of a given era, art being the expression of the spirit of a nation. In Russia, however, they also reflected the tastes of her monarchs up until the early nineteenth century. During Catherine the Great's reign, for example, there was immense progress due to her efforts. She succeeded in locating and buying all of the architect Clériseau's portfolios of drawings he had made during his time in Italy, which included detailed sketches of that county's massive vase construction methods and other guides to aid the various arts. She placed orders for porcelains with most of Europe's major factories, among the more important of which was one for a massive dinner service from Meissen, the famous Hunter Service, on each piece of which a different hunting scene was painted. She delighted in Wedgwood and became one of his most valued clients. She used these porcelains as touchstones for her porcelain decorators and modelers. Quality was adhered to meticulously; the Russians' one problem was that the whiteness achieved in the German products could not be matched because the blue tint that exists in Russian kaolin could not be eradicated.

Catherine's son, the unbalanced but politically astute Paul I (1796–1801), continued with his detested mother's promotion of the arts, and of porcelain in particular. The painting of flowers excelled during his reign. In 1799 he was responsible for the founding of a small extension of the Imperial Porcelain Factory close to his favorite residence, the Gatchina

---

*The Soviet porcelain which is produced for the Urdu-speaking market is often marked with this red mark. The St. George, however, upon close inspection, is replaced by the hammer and sickle, and at other times by the crescent.

Palace, some thirty-five miles south of St. Petersburg. His unexpected and frequent visits were known to hinder production there. On the day before his assassination he received a completed dinner service that he had commissioned, and is said to have exclaimed that it was the happiest day of his life.

The reign of Paul's son, Alexander I (1801–25), saw the apogee of Classicism in Russia, with the porcelain factories playing a contributory role. Among the new men who were brought to Russia during this time was one of the more important porcelain decorators of the age, Schverbakh. He had worked at Sèvres for twelve years and its influence is clearly discernible in his work. As France enjoyed depictions of Napoleon's victories on their porcelain, so did Russia of hers, and in 1815 when he arrived to work in that country, he simply transferred his talents to the painting of Russian, instead of French, uniforms. This vogue for romantically presented battle scenes and dashing officers in resplendent uniforms, sometimes with their magnificent chargers, grew in popularity—a popularity which continued in future reigns. The production of figurines also continued into future reigns; those that were made during that of Alexander I may be distinguished by a dull underglazed blue which predominated in their decoration.

A further decorative style for porcelain in Alexander's day took the form of gilding, with all the greater factories and their decorators lavishly embellishing work that included renditions of paintings by such artists as Orlovsky, Venetsianov and others of similar romantic persuasion. Low relief with fanciful intertwining of leaves, flower heads and scrollwork in color was also popular. The great Arabesque Service was produced in 1784, with the assistance of Schverbakh. The Yacht Service commemorating Russian victories over the Turks also exemplifies the excellence of Russian workmanship at that time.

Starkly black silhouettes upon white grounds were a further feature of this reign's tastes. In order to safeguard the porcelain industry, the ever practical Alexander issued a decree placing a prohibitive tariff on the import of foreign porcelain into the country, which stimulated domestic production and resulted in a similar embargo being placed upon the import of glass, and later on textiles.

With the advent of Nicholas I, a gradual decline in tastes set in, with neo-Gothic and pseudomedieval Russian scenes coming into favor. Wood carving and malachite were often simulated on porcelain decoration; the pieces were heavy, though cleverly executed. The latter part of this emperor's reign produced some of the most exquisite porcelain ever to have been manufactured in Russia. This *pièce de résistance* consisted of several series of plates dedicated to various regiments, on which officers and men in full dress, as well as in field uniforms, were depicted. The miniatures were painted by such artists as Piratsky and Kirsanov on surfaces which measured only between eight and ten inches in diameter; and on the completion of each plate the artist's name was placed on its reverse side together with the date. The borders of the plates were decorated with various delicately painted, gilt military trophies, sometimes with laurel leaves or floral swags and/or scrolls. Two-headed eagles often surmount the designs, or the date of the battle encircled by laurel wreaths and battle trophies. In 1851 the Imperial Porcelain Factory received a gold medal at the Crystal Palace Exhibition in London for the Military Series.

Similar plates were produced in later reigns, all of which are avidly collected today when, very occasionally, they appear at auction; the results of sale prices vary depending upon which type of plate is sold, for some of them were more lavishly decorated than others. It is not unusual for them to realize some £5,000 a piece today.

With the coming of Alexander III's reign (1881–94), most of the porcelain industry went into an inexplicable decline. It was not only the artistry that suffered, but the skills of craftsmen were also affected. Articles were produced that were malformed, glazings were often singed, colors were uninspired, uneven and discolored. A rich cobalt blue (in the style of the *bleu de Sèvres*) became fashionable, especially for tea sets, and the delicate miniatures of the past were replaced by crude flower pictures, usually in cartouche form. The general deterioration in taste that had manifested itself in mid-century intensified. The days when the monarchs' preferences were of paramount importance were over.

However, as his grandfather's reign saw the appearance of the prize-winning military plates, Alexander III's produced its own *chef d'oeuvre* when the Imperial Porcelain Factory produced the Raphael Service. In her time Catherine the Great had Sancio Raphael's Vatican logia duplicated in its entirety at one end of the Winter Palace (in the annex she built as a private residence called the Hermitage, which Nicholas I turned into a museum). The Imperial Porcelain Factory, taking it as its theme, produced this magnificently imaginative and detailed porcelain service, with exquisitely painted friezes and medallions.

The initials of the reigning monarchs serve as date marks on the bases of all articles emerging from the Imperial Porcelain Factory, providing a simple method for the recognition of a piece's date of production. See the chart for marks that distinguished the very early items of production in Elizabethan Russia, together with some of the more important other marks. Without a thorough knowledge of these, very little can be accomplished by the collector. Instinctive recognition only comes with time and experience.

Under the last Romanov tsar, Nicholas II (1894–1917), subject matter in porcelain decoration became more diversified, and the quality of production improved immeasurably. Easter eggs were produced in great numbers, many of which were of a tremendous beauty—their significance will be discussed in a coming chapter. The reproduction of landscapes for decorative purposes returned to favor, and paintings by Levitan and Nesterov were frequently copied. Among the more successful pieces that the Imperial Porcelain Factory executed was a model taken from Valentin Serov's painting of *Europa and the Bull*. After the Revolution of 1917 this group was reproduced many times from the old molds. One such undecorated model was found by the author for £5 in an open London market; on the base the factory mark of Nicholas II's crowned cypher had been crudely erased and replaced by a hammer and sickle. Such alterations are often found

	The Imperial Porcelain Factory The marks from the reigns of the Empress Elizabeth and Peter III
	CATHERINE II ('Ekatirina'), 'the Great'
	PAUL
	ALEXANDER I
	NICHOLAS I
	ALEXANDER II
	ALEXANDER III
	NICHOLAS II
	THE GARDNER FACTORY (The later Gardner mark, usually in red.)
	THE POPOV FACTORY
	THE KUZNETZOV FACTORY
	THE FACTORY OF THE BROTHERS KORNILOV

on objects that appear on the markets of the West today; porcelain fashioned by the old regime has been latterly decorated by Soviet artists. These marks, in themselves, are of interest to collectors because of their historic connotations.

In the years immediately preceding the Revolution of 1917, the Imperial Factory was headed by the author Baron de Wolf, who wrote extensively on the subject of his stewardship. He occupied the post until 1910, at which time N. Stroukhov became the factory's final Director. For patriotic reasons during the war years (1914–17) production was purely utilitarian at the Imperial Porcelain Factory. In 1918–23, and in 1925–27, a former member of the Mir Iskusstva (the World of Art movement), the artist Sergei Tchekhonin was appointed as Artistic Director of what had become the State Porcelain Factory.

Following the traumatic days of the 1917 Revolution and the resulting Civil War that lasted into the early twenties, the various industries of Russia or, as it had become, the R.S.S.R. (Russian Soviet Socialist Republic) gradually resumed production despite inevitable difficulties. The State Porcelain Factory Director, an artist of outstanding talent with interests like those of many of his contemporary artists, was affected by politics which reflected in production, and thus "propaganda porcelain" came into being.

The initial work at the various factories was crude and uninspired, but its decoration was often of first caliber because many of the *avant-garde* artists followed Tchekhonin's lead and contributed their work to this particular industry; Kasimir Malevich, for example, not only decorated many items, but designed them in his own favored Suprematist style.

It is interesting to note that today's sales of Imperial and post-revolutionary Russian procelain are not illustrated in descriptive literature with artifacts from the past's dazzling production, but with Soviet propaganda porcelain. Historic value naturally contributes to commercial value. A Soviet propoganda dish called *The Bell Ringer,* after a design by the Russo-Polish artist Shchikotikina-Pototska, dated 1921, sold for £20,900 at Christie's (London) recently.

In February to April of 1989 an important exhibition took place at the Lakeview Museum of Arts and Science in Peoria, Illinois. Some fifty representative pieces from the Raymond F. Piper Collection of Imperial Russian porcelain were on display. The exhibition covered the period of the Imperial Factory's entire production. Mr. Piper has assembled the collection not only for aesthetic reasons but also for educative purposes; it shows the stunning virtuosity of technical development in the Russian porcelain industry.

The work-masters' marks.

B.A.	Johan Victor Aarne		М.П.	Mikhail Pershin
Ф.A.	Fedor Afanassiev		I.P.	Julius Rappoport
G.A.	Carl Gustave Hjalmar Armfelt		W.R.	Wilhem Reimer
A.Г.	Andrei Gorainov		Ф.P.	Fedor Rükert
A.H.	Anguste Wilhelm Holström		B.C.	Vladimir Soloviev
A.H.	Auguste Frederik Hollming		A.T.	Alfred Thielman
E.K.	Erik Auguste Kollin		H.W.	Hendrik Wigström
A.N.	Anders Johan Nevelainen		A.W.	Alexandre Wäkewä
G.N.	Gabriel Niukkanen		S.W.	Stephan Wäkewä

(Prospective collectors should always carry this list with them—just in case!)

The collecting of Russian porcelain has been referred to in the Introduction and there is very little to add to what has already been said. It is necessary for the collector to familiarize him/herself with the various manufactories' work and styles of production, the patterns and subject matter with which the porcelain is decorated, identifying marks, and types of paste that were used: Russian porcelain, as has been said, never achieved the whiteness of Meissen's output because Russian clay is of a different composition. Russian kaolin was always used in Russian porcelain; the Empress Elizabeth Petrovna had stipulated that she would promote its production providing that her country's earth was used exclusively in its manufacture.

A number of specialist books exist on the subject for a collector's initial guidance and reference purposes.

CHAPTER SEVEN

Glasshouses

*I*t is often said in the West that Russian glass and crystal objects that have any age or quality to them are, in fact, products of Germany or Bohemia. This is not the case. Although these countries did, indeed, produce articles for Russian and other markets of the world, glasshouses existed in Russia for many centuries. Historical records give details of a great many such establishments that were operational from the seventeenth century on; clearly there must have been glasshouses at an earlier date, for glass, enamels and mosaics existed in pre-Tartar Kievan Rus, but due to the country's turbulent medieval history, little or nothing appears to be known about them.

It is quite extraordinary how much antique Russian glass can be found in Western Europe and in America today. It has survived the years remarkably well considering its fragility. The story of Russian glassmaking is just as full of adventure as that of porcelain.

When in 1472 the widowed Ivan III married the exiled Byzantine Emperor's niece Sophia Paléologue, her dowry contained a collection of glass plates decorated with two-headed Byzantine eagles. The Tsar decided that the eagles' posture with one head looking to the east and the other to the west was the perfect symbol for his vast domains. The eagles established themselves in Russian motifs and retained a role until the fall of the Romanov dynasty in 1917, at which time they were replaced by the hammer and sickle.

Strangely, considering their beauty, no reproductions were ever made of the Tsaritza Sophia's plates, other than some green and gold ones that carry patterns of somewhat similar design made by the Imperial Porcelain Factory during the reign of Nicholas I (1826).

In 1637 a Swede, Elias "Koët, set up a glass manufactory at Mojhaisk and another within the Kremlin walls at about the same time. State-owned glasshouses were established in the village of Ismailov in 1668 and at the Sparrow Hills, near Moscow, in 1705; they were closed down in 1713 and reopened under private ownership. Two more factories appeared in 1725, one at Vladimir, the other at Moscow, both of which specialized in window glass, although it is recorded that decorative objects were made also. In 1719 another glasshouse was founded by A. Minter in the region of Dmitrov, and it is known to have produced 145,000 glass objects, but the duration of its operation is not known.

Vassili Malzev was an eighteenth-century proprietor of a glasshouse near Moscow; his business prospered and he opened additional factories as time progressed. One of Malzev's factories is known as Guz-Khroustalny Zavod, which is the center of glass production in the Soviet Union today. Further glass manufactories were located at Yamburg and Jhabino and a few existed in and around St. Petersburg. In the eighteenth century the opening of the great Ust Ruditskaya and Shlisselberg works was signifi-cent.

This brief outline clearly shows that there was a good deal of activity in this particular field of the arts in Russia.

The Imperial glassworks in St. Petersburg came into being during the reign of the Empress Elizabeth, and she carried her father's enthusiasm for innovation into the mid-eighteenth century. She encouraged production at her glass factories by placing large orders for goblets, sweetmeat dishes, decanters and kvass jugs, saltcellers with lids, wineglasses and vases. These commissions, naturally, were emulated by those of her subjects who could afford to do so, causing increased production, progress and prosperity.

Glass is seldom marked with an identifying stamp of production, but sometimes the letters П.К.(P.K.), *Predvornaya Kantora* which stands for the Imperial Crown Office, can be found scratched on an article's base.★ Such pieces are often decorated with crowned Imperial cyphers, with each monarch's personal cypher identifying the reign during which a piece was made.

In the late seventeenth century and at the beginning of the eighteenth, colorless glass was manufactured in abundance, especially rectangular decanters, beakers, wineglasses and goblets. These items were engraved with diverse motifs: with emblems, battle trophies, idyllic scenes, crests—and, as has been said, items that carried crowned cyphers or simply the Arms of State, were produced for use in palaces, on specific occasions and for presentation as gifts to foreign dignitaries.

The earliest eighteenth century glasses were comparatively simple in design, with only one or two knops on the baluster stems, and a similar number of knops decorating the lids, but very little of the latter survived the years. With the century's advance, glass became more ornate, the engraving more complicated, and the wineglasses and goblets developed more knops on their stems. Apart from engraving, which was sometimes picked out in black and gold, the only other decoration that was carried by these wares consisted of gold or colored threads introduced into the stems, and air bubbles occasionally in the lower stems. Later, glass was decorated with enamels, and wineglasses with small shields cemented to them which bore inscriptions, flowers, crests or cyphers; these shields or plaques are usually white, navy blue or maroon, and the decoration is gold. (e.g., The Alexandrine Service of Alexander I.)

★The Crown Office, or the Office of H.I.M's Cabinet, controlled the Privy Purse, and all things belonging and pertaining to the Crown. It was inaugurated by Peter I.

In the year 1747 all glasshouses and foundries were ordered to close in Moscow and other densely populated areas for fear of fire. State owned glasshouses were transferred to sites adjacent to the newly built St. Petersburg. One glasshouse, however, is known to have existed on the banks of the Fontanka Canal in St. Petersburg until the 1770s.

By the 1850s all State-owned glasshouses had merged to become the Imperial Glass Manufactory which ranked first in importance, and turned out beautiful objects for the Crown, the State and for people with monied tastes. It was closely followed in importance by the Malzev and the Bakhmetiev glasshouses.

During the second half of the eighteenth century, Bakhmetiev opened a glasshouse in the village of Nikolsk in the district of Penza; at the end of that century his heirs owned three establishments (he died in 1779). One of these factories produced high quality crystal, while others specialized in sheet glass and inexpensive wares. In 1802 the Bakhmetiev manufactory's production amounted to approximately 45,000 rubles, a considerable sum of money at that time.

As technical knowledge increased so did the novelties of production. Various types of glass enjoyed fashionable moments, and during the course of the eighteenth century an amusing object called a glass sandwich came into being; it is an object which is avidly collected today as it is of the greatest rarity. For its production two glass bowls were made; the outside of the inner bowl was covered with gold or silver foil onto which designs were scratched; it was then fitted into the outer bowl, and the sandwich was then ready for further decoration. Russian sandwiches show traces of the pontil mark, while they are seldom found on Bohemian glass.

Colored glass became popular and made its initial appearance during the first half of the eighteenth century in Russia. Understandably the colors were initially dull, mottled and murky, but gradually they improved and various shades of violet, red, blue, milky white (which incorporated ground bones), turquoise, and a bright emerald green were achieved. Colored glass was seldom engraved in Russia. As a rule it was painted with garlands of acanthus, flowers, ships, battle and idyllic scenes, or simply with designs in cartouche form. Colored glass, or smalt (pulverized glass used as a pigment for coloring matter) was used in mosaics; the word *mosaic,* in Russia, was synonymous with the name of Lomonossov.

In the year 1711, Mikhail Vassilievich Lomonossov was born into a comfortably situated peasant family that lived in a village called Denisovka, located on the White Sea close to Kholmogory in the country's extreme north. He was brought up as any child of his background—he ran and played with other children, he helped his father with the fishing and he read avidly: his thirst for knowledge was insatiable. In the end this thirst led the local people, and the father of Russia's greatest sculptor, Fedot Shubin, to take up a collection to send young Lomonossov to Moscow to seek his fortune. In 1730 he entered the Slavonic-Greco-Latin Academy where he acquired a fluency in Latin and studied philosophy. He also studied at Kiev, but he ended his years of tuition at Marburg, in Germany, coincidentally in the company of Dmitri Vinogradov, the inventor of Russia's true porcelain. On his return to Russia he was appointed to the Academy of Sciences.

Lomonossov's renown grew quickly, for his prowess and brilliant inventiveness in all spheres of academic learning led to international recognition of his genius. In addition, his prose and poetry were of so high a standard that he is accused of having changed the Russian language. He set a standard for the formidable coterie of nineteenth-century writers—Pushkin, Krylov, Tioutchev and Turgeniev, Dostoevsky, Chekhov and Tolstoy and the others. In his spare time he indulged in his second interest (the first was writing and documentation), the art of mosaic.

In 1751 the Academy of Sciences was requested by the Ministry of the Interior to loan Lomonossov to the Imperial Glasshouse to help them perfect the technique of producing colored glass. No doubt with Lomonossov's enthusiastic consent, the request was granted, for he was then conducting experiments into optics for which colored glass is a necessity. He was sent to the factory's laboratory where he proceeded to instruct and to develop his inventions. He trained Petr Droujhinin, a gifted technician, in the art of melting glass and the enamel process; this man became a master craftsman.* The fifties saw unprecedented achievement, for among this scientist's and thinker's gifts was an energy which drove him beyond the average man's capacities. In time Lomonossov was obliged to return to the Academy, despite the fact that there were certain hues still necessary for his experiments which had not yet been perfected.

Lomonossov requested and received a plot of land not far from St. Petersburg on which he built a small factory which employed sixty people. He named it Ust Rudinskaya. Production commenced in 1754, permitting Lomonossov to conduct all the experiments that were necessary for his research. He fashioned a number of pictures in mosaic, concentrating on portraiture and topography, and not iconography. He was responsible for the monumental picture of *The Battle of Poltava,* which is fifteen feet high by twenty feet in length, and took four years to complete. Another huge mosaic, *The Surrender of Azov,* remains unfinished. They are both at the Academy of Sciences.

In his work Lomonossov used large pieces of tesserae, preferring them to the smaller ones which the Italians favored. His colors are less delicate than those of the Italians, but his work was venturesome, and he experimented with many novel techniques in the art of mosaics. Lomonossov's studio on the Moica canal (in Saint Petersburg) did not survive him for long, for mosaic as an art form was not popular in Russia other than for table and floor decoration. He once laid a mosaic floor himself in the Chinese Palace's Glass Study at Oranienbaum, which today is called Lomonossov in his honor, but the floor did not survive the years. Some of his table tops, which were a combination of glass tesserae and marble, have fortunately been preserved.

Catherine the Great visited Lomonossov at his studio in 1764 and spent

---

*Among the experiments and investigations that were conducted by both Lomonossov and Droujhinin into the problems of creating varied forms of glass and its decoration were: the crizzling defects; *eglomisé* glass decorations; ice glass procedures; iridescence in glass; milk and opaque glass; optical glass; filigree or *à la façon de Venise* glass, which contains threads of embedded glass; the gilding of glass; layered or double walled glass (the sandwich); enameling of glass; the use of sulphides; acid etching.

several hours examining his mosaics, inventions and writings. A description of her visit was recorded by him in his diary for posterity. Lomonossov died in 1775 inexplicably, in penury.

During the late eighteenth and early nineteenth centuries the Imperial Glasshouses began to produce cut and faceted crystal of high quality which became popular and fashionable. Massive chandeliers and torchères were produced, often married to malachite and other mineral parts, as well as to fire-gilt bronze, with dazzling effects, in what came to be known as "the Russian style." Such combinations of materials were greatly favored, and objects of clear, colored or opaque glass were often found carrying gilt-bronze handles and other such decorations, reposing upon plinths of semi-precious stone from the Ural and the Altai mountain ranges. Catherine the Great especially favored vast porcelain and glass columns and vases.

Between the years 1782–87 the Scottish architect Charles Cameron built for Catherine a small house on the grounds at Tsarskoye Selo (today's Pushkin), which she named the Agate Pavilion. Its style was based on the lines of both Grecian and Roman architecture with a semi-circular Ionic gallery joining two pavilions. This gem of architectural prowess was replete with "Russian style" decoration: it was also filled with an ever increasing collection of bronze busts of her *vremenshchiki* (short time lovers)—a whimsical touch which proclaims her unquestionable sense of humor. In the Catherine Palace at Tsarskoye Selo (named for Catherine I, not the Great), today's Pushkin, Cameron installed a glass ceiling of vast dimensions: drawing upon Adam's plans for Kedlestone in England, and on Clérisseau for inspiration, he created the Cabinet of Mirrors, in which the walls are covered with milky glass and decorated with bronze eagles and sphinxes. The Tabatière Room also contains glass walls, numerous mirrors and bronze decoration, to which he added violet glass columns and Wedgwood plaques. The specialist in glass craftsmanship with whom Cameron worked was a German, König, and the production of mirrors, plates of glass and the columns to Cameron's design, must be ascribed to his hand.

From the seventeenth century, Russia went through the same process of artistic development as other European countries. The colorless glass of the eighteenth century was replaced by colorless lead crystal, the engraving of glass by cutting and faceting. The development of mass production in the arts brought many things within financial reach of the common people. The Alexandrine era initiated the beginings of the end of social privileges and certain injustices. The era of French enlightenment began to yield its fruits.

Alexander's liking for glass and crystal is not known, but it is known that he disliked ostentation. He was, however, generous in the gifts that he presented, particularly to foreigners, for this he did on behalf of Russia. At the conclusion of the Russo–Persian War in 1813 his policy was to maintain peace with the Shah, to whom he presented a wondrous crystal bath in 1818. The jubilant Shah's immediate response was a request for a crystal bed as a companion piece. Whether this request was complied with or not is unknown.

The Imperial Glass Manufactory experienced many changes of ownership during the course of its existence. Peter the Great once presented it to his friend Prince Menshikov, but with his arrest and disgrace, it was confiscated and returned to the State. Catherine the Great made a gift of it to her lover, Prince Potemkin of Tauride; after his death she bought it back from his heirs. In 1890 the Imperial Glass Manufactory was merged with the Imperial Porcelain Factory by Imperial decree.

No highly specialized knowledge is required for collecting Russian glass. The interested person should be familiar with the various emblems, cyphers and likenesses of personages who were often in the engravings. The recognition of specifically Russian shapes and forms should also be mastered.

The arrangement of glass for display purposes is really a matter of personal taste and preference. A well-lit display cabinet is the safest lodging place, particularly if children and/or animals are present. Glass should always be kept in pristine condition, washed, rubbed very dry and sparkling. No liquid should be kept in ancient glass as it can create an indelible ring; glassware can become "sick," a condition that is very difficult to eradicate.

CHAPTER EIGHT

Jewelry and the Goldsmiths

Self adornment and the possession of precious things have always been human weaknesses, so the progress of the goldsmith and the jeweler in the lands which today constitute Greater Russia and the Ukraine was less traumatic for the practitioners than of other art forms. It is, therefore, with interest and a certain awe that we view the various artifacts that come to light when ancient *kourgans* (burial mounds) are excavated, and astonishment and disbelief when the level of sophistication that existed so many centuries ago is revealed.

The Hermitage Museum in Leningrad holds a collection of some of the rarest items that the *kourgans* have disclosed, items such as a Scythian golden fibula in the form of a panther from the sixth century B.C.; a silver plaque with an embossed eagle seizing a lamb from the fifth century B.C. *Kourgan of the Seven Brothers;* a pierced bronze plaque depicting two bulls in confrontation from the third century B.C., which was found at Kopterevo in 1890. A fine-toothed, fourth century B.C. golden comb with exquisite decoration across the top was unearthed in southern Russia shortly before the Revolution.

Kolty, which are peculiar to Slav territories, are frequently found; they are pendants fashioned to contain textile soaked in perfume and often decorated with the Sirin and Alconist motifs, which were worn by women over the brow or temples.* Huge drinking horns from the tenth century B.C. were discovered in the *Black Kourgan* in the region of Chernigov. Long, intricately wrought chains of precious metals have been excavated; *narouchi,* which are very wide bracelets that served to hold sleeves in at the wrists and amulets, small idols of deities, rings, bracelets and necklaces, bowls and daggers with ornamental handles, and carved ivory items have been found over the years, predominently in southern Russia—some in the Red Ochre Graves of two thousand years B.C.

These treasures are decorated with much the same motifs as were the early embroideries and carvings, with the dot and comma patterns of the Scythians as well as the intrinsically Slav geometric floral and scroll designs, animals, ducks, swans, and peacocks, eagles, horses, bulls and antlered stags. Later, historical events added their influences when the Varangian, Byzantine, Caucasian and Persian arts intruded into those of Russia. The various motifs were interwoven with one another over the centuries to form patterns which, like jigsaws, provide entertaining problems when historians seek to determine centuries of origin.

In the late tenth century when Christianity came to Rus from the Byzantine Empire, it was accompanied by many subsidiary influences, among which was fashion. The strangely ascetic, heavy jewelry greatly favored by the early Greeks and various Hellenistic designs were adapted as decorations for Kievan metalwork and items of personal adornment. Metalwork was richly set with pearls, precious and semi-precious stones in the Greek manner, but niellowork, glass and enameling were already

---

*Sirin and Alconist were two half-bird half-woman creatures of ancient legend, who sang so sweetly that they were permitted to live in Paradise to enchant its inhabitants.

known to the Slavs and had been widely used in pre-Christian times for both religious and secular purposes. Filigree and lacy patterns which are achieved from malleable metals were also known in Kievan Rus. As we know during the second decade of the thirteenth century the Golden Horde ravaged and looted central and southern Russia. Items made from precious metals were melted down and almost all evidence of a progressive and fascinating past was destroyed.

By the mid-sixteenth century, Russia's subjugation to the Horde had ended, and the country was shaking off the final vestiges of Greek influence (in all but iconography, church music and ritual). There was a great upsurge in all areas of the arts. Moscow, which by this time had matured and had received the central government into its environs, took from Novgorod the role of being the cultural center of the land. Its rulers had assumed the title of Tsar; the lifestyles of the Court, nobles, prosperous merchants and certain urban dwellers were lavish. When Richard Chancellor "stumbled" on Russia on his way to seek a northern route to Cathay for Elizabeth I of England, he was amazed and dazzled by the amount of ceremony and splendor, as well as of gold plate, that he saw on display when he was invited to Court by the then Tsar Ivan the Terrible. The later Tsar Boris Godunov's love for luxury and beauty is known fact. He promoted art projects of the most recherché variety and was responsible for the exquisite *Pearl Palena* for Andrei Rublev's icon of the *Old Testament Trinity*. He and the Boyarin Mikhail Romanov presented a magnificent gold icon cover, or *riza,* for the same icon, which was encrusted with precious stones: the central angel's halo contains a particularly splendid emerald. It was the work of an unnamed Venetian jeweler who worked for Godunov exclusively at that time. Godunov's death in 1605 was followed by the Troubled Times, but 1613 saw the arrival of the Romanov dynasty, and the dawning of a new and exiting era for Russia.

During the years of the early Romanovs the arts continued to progress, guided by the vicissitudes of fashion. Western influences encroached in full force during the seventeenth century, when many artists and craftsmen brought to Russia their countries' art forms and techniques. Metal workers also came, but this was an area in which foreigners could teach the Russians very little that was new, for the metal industry as well as that of the lapidary and jeweler, had attained high standards by that time.

Until the seventeenth century the hallmarking of precious metals had been highly erratic, with principalities, and later governments (counties) using identifying crests that were roughly and often haphazardly applied. In 1700, Peter the Great, as in so many other fields, introduced standards and systematic methods for the identification of precious metals. In 1785, Catherine the Great inaugurated even more sophisticated methods, and the coveted status of Master Craftsman became less easily available. By 1793, three years before her death, there were some fifty master craftsmen in St. Petersburg; by the early nineteenth century, however, the number had risen to 150.

Platinum received no specific hallmarks and was often mistaken for silver. Early Russian silver, therefore, should always be examined carefully in order to establish its true composition. Russian silver does not have the same purity of content as does Western silver. The standards are described by the number of *zolotniks** of pure silver in ninety-six parts, and the numerals 84, 88 and 91 describe the content. Gold is represented by the numerals 56, 72 and 92, again, in relation to ninety-six *zolotniks*.

Finally it was decreed that four regulation marks were to be applied at all times. First, the initials of the assay master; second, the crest of the town in which the article was tested, not necessarily made; third, the hallmark describing the content as explained above; fourth, the workmaster's initials or full name; and together with these marks a date mark is often found. A tiny equestrian figure of St. George stands for Moscow, and crossed anchors centered by a scepter, St. Petersburg. In the early eighteenth century the eagles of State preceded the crossed anchors representing St. Petersburg, as they did on the Imperial Porcelain Factory's wares before a reigning monarch's crowned cypher came to replace them.

---

*A *zolotnik* is described by the *Oxford Russian-English Dictionary* as "an old Russian measure of weight equivalent to 1/96 of Russian pound." 36 pounds constituted one *pud*.

The Emperor Alexander III with his favorite coachman in an informal winter sleigh. Signed and dated by Nicholas Sverchkov, 1891. (*Courtesy of the former Bowater Gallery*)

Small, enamelled beaker with handle; glass goblet with the crowned eagle of State, an Imperial cypher is on the reverse side —eighteenth century; two silver and enamel vodka cups; chocolate cup and saucer with lid —Imperial Porcelain Factory —the miniature is of Alexander I. (*Courtesy of the former Bowater Gallery*)

A collection of Russian enamelled silver objects, nineteenth century.
(*Courtesy of the former Bowater Gallery*)

At rear are two plates and a cup and saucer from the Imperial Porcelain Factory; figure of a peasant girl bearing the mark of the Popov Factory, mid-nineteenth century; the porcelain egg, Imperial Porcelain Factory, bears the crowned cypher of the Empress Alexandra Fedorovna; malachite box with agate in its lid, nineteenth century; a large brass Orthodox Crucifixion with enamel decoration, nineteenth century; a circular ivory box with carved head of Catherine II as Minerva, eighteenth century; a small circular silver/enamel box, nineteenth century; an enamelled silver vodka cup in the shape of a *kaska* (helmet) standing on its rim, by Carl Fabergé, nineteenth century; an eighteenth century enamelled icon container. (*Courtesy of the former Bowater Gallery*)

A porcelain figurine of a peasant-vendor by the Gardner, Factory, nineteenth century; a bronze group of a mounted peasant lassoing a cow,
nineteenth century by Eugène Lanceré; an eighteenth century goblet
bearing the Imperial eagle; a double silver chain interspersed with
enamel beads, nineteenth century. *Front Row:* a silver crucifixion, nineteenth century, a white porcelain Easter egg with the Empress Alexandra Fedorovna's crowned cypher; a medal of St. Vladimir, with swords,
gold; a biscuit figure of a seated peasant drinking from a barrel, nineteenth century Gardner Factory; a pair of officer's epaulets (or
"boards") bearing the crowned cipher of Nicholas II. (*Courtesy of the former Bowater Gallery*)

A group of Russian bronzes by Gratchov and Lanceré. The latter's *Cossak's Farewell to his Girl* is on top right, nineteenth century. (*Courtesy of the former Bowater Gallery*)

The Author's first gallery in Kensington, London. (*Courtesy of the former Bowater Gallery*)

A seventeenth century "pocket sized" icon of the Birth of Christ —note the star: brass. A rare seventeenth century enamelled brass icon. (*Courtesy of the former Bowater Gallery*)

A silver goblet with varied designs, Moscow, dated 1834; a figurine of a peasant woman standing on a round base which indicates later, nineteenth century production —Imperial Factory; a brass *nadvershoye* (a standard top). *Below:* a bronze bear sprawled on a piece of malachite. (*Courtesy of the former Bowater Gallery*)

A seventeenth century Russian head-dress of red velvet and embroidered with river pearls; a later nineteenth century figurine of a peasant lad, Gardner Factory; a set of six silver vodka cups; a round, eighteenth century box bearing the head of Catherine II as Minerva. *Left to right:* a delightful crouching figure in gilt bronze which holds two containers —for ink and for sand, early nineteenth century, the base is of "crushed velvet" malachite. A small, nineteenth century triptych icon; a miniature of Alexander I, unknown painter; a bronze bear on a crystal base, nineteenth century. (*Courtesy of the former Bowater Gallery*)

A portrait of a Georgian woman by Vladimir Makovsky (1846-1920).
The artist was the son of a well known collector Igor Makovsky, and the
brother of his equally well known artist, Konstantin. Both the brothers
taught at the Academy of Arts. (*Courtesy of the former Bowater Gallery*)

A figurine of a coachman, Imperial Factory, mid-nineteenth century; a silver salt container, with a narrow *champlevé*, enamelled design round the side, Ovchinnikov Factory, nineteenth century; a miniature of Nicholas I, artisit unknown, in an ivory frame —the surmounting eagles' wings, however, are not of this reign's design which suggests later workmanship. A seated figurine of a *boublichki* (bun) vendor, biscuit, Gardner Factory, second half of the nineteenth century; a rare Chamberlain's Key (a badge of office) in bronze, nineteenth century. (*Courtesy of the former Bowater Gallery*)

A collection of Russian silver *lampadas* (oil burning light containers), which are centered by a censer. The collection is set against the background of a portable, eighteenth century *iconostasis*. (*Courtesy of the former Bowater Gallery*)

Two plates from the *Military Series*. Nicholas I period, Imperial Porcelain Factory. (*Courtesy of the former Bowater Gallery*)

An excellent quality, eighteenth century portable *iconostasis*. It consists of fourteen panels which close in upon the central one upon which the Tsar Gates are represented. (*Courtesy of the former Bowater Gallery*)

An icon of St. Nicholas the Wondermaker covered with a rich and heavily worked silver *riza*; small icons of Christ and the Mother of God are (always) to the right and left of his head, nineteenth century. An icon of the Mother and Child in a richly worked silver *basma* —the picture is left exposed, the neutral areas is covered with silver, nineteenth century. (*Courtesy of the former Bowater Gallery*)

A small oil painting of a peasant lad wearing *lapti*, by Venetzianov
(1780-1847). This painting was found in an open London market for
£5 during the 1960s. Unsigned. (*Courtesy of the former Bowater Gallery*)

An excellent miniature of Alexander I by an unknown artist. He wears the officer's white enamel medal of St. George amongst others. (*Courtesy of the former Bowater Gallery*)

A collection of Russian papier mâché, with a table snuffbox of Karelian birch which is inset with the Imperial Eagle, nineteenth century. (*Courtesy of the former Bowater Gallery*)

A collection of small papier mâché boxes, nineteenth century. *Top Left:* a rare box carrying a topographical scene; the body of it is decorated with silver dots and trellis work. Another snuff box with a delightful miniature after Venetzianov. Two table snuff boxes with inset portraits of Emperors. A match box with a balalaika player. A box with a dashing summer troika. (*Courtesy of the former Bowater Gallery*)

Three examples of Russian *cloisonné* enamelling. The two traditional *kovshes* have the hooked handles and lobed bodies with varie colored scrolls and blossoms, which are further embellished with raised pellets decorating them, as they do the box; nineteenth century. (*Courtesy of the former Bowater Gallery*)

The Yaroslavl Virgin. This particular version of the Mother of God and her Child is of the fifteenth century Moscow school. It is an icon of *Oumileniye* —of tenderness —and it shows a well painted, playful Christ-Child sitting on His mother's arm and protected by her maphorion (her veil). The stars on her forehead and shoulders indicate her perpetual virginity —before, during and after the Child's birth. *(Courtesy of Tretiakov Gallery)*

A seventeenth century icon of *Christ Pantocrator*, Moscow school. The beautifully worked silver *riza* is of similar date as the icon. (*Courtesy of Christie's*)

A collection of nineteenth century Russian wooden items. The salt chair on left is finely carved with floral motifs, on bracket feet. (*Courtesy of Christie's*)

A portrait of Alexandre Sergeyevich Pushkin, the poet, by Petr Fe-
dorovich Sokolov (1791-1848), which was painted in c. 1830. 8½ x 6¾
inches. Pencil, pen and black ink and watercolor heightened with
white on paper. This picture recently fetched £44,000 pounds at Christies, possibly not for Sokolov's work, which is masterly, but for its being of Pushkin. (*Courtesy of Christie's*)

A collection of top quality papier mâché pieces by the Loukutin and the Vishniakov factories. The napkin ring carries the Kremlin round its circumference; the second napkin ring and the matchbox holder are decorated by peasant figures; the snuff box is of Karelian birch; the portrait is of Peter the Great, nineteenth century. (*Courtesy of Christie's*)

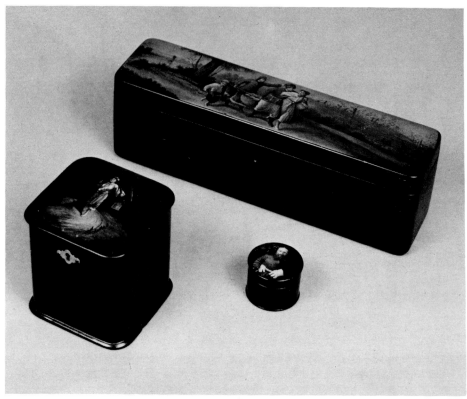

These three further examples of Lukoutin and Vishniakov workmanship are a glovebox, a tea caddy and a small pill box, nineteenth century. (*Courtesy of Christie's*)

A draughtsboard and "men" in papier mâché, nineteenth century. The black pieces are boxes with pictures of men, the white pieces consist of white papier mâché boxes with depictions of peasant women, nineteenth century. (*Courtesy of Christies*)

An amusing nineteenth century parody of a *kovsh*. The tail handle is replaced by a carved man's head, but the traditional bird's-head remains a feature. The wood is carved and painted with branches and flower-heads. (*Courtesy of Sotheby's*)

In 1896 a minute woman's head wearing a *kokoshnik* replaced the town's arms and date of production.

The splendid Empresses who dominated Russia in the eighteenth century were far from backward in promoting and supporting the jewelers' art. But this particular industry really stood in no need of assistance because the life of society's upper strata provided sufficient demand for the jewelers' services to maintain a healthy state in their affairs.

Life at the Courts of these Empresses was a constant round of entertainments in Versailles-like settings. There were weekly balls and pageants, State functions, dinners and diplomatic receptions. The fact that the most important and weighty negotiations and decisons often took place at a balle masqué or in a boudoir, for example, is forgotten, but, nonetheless, all these events were occasions for self-adornment. Diamond ribbons–strips of cloth to which diamonds were permanently fixed, were used for threading through ladies' wigs, as well as for decorating successive garments. Diamonds and other jewels adorned shoe buckles, belts and swords; they blazed from ears, throats and bosoms, aide-mémoires, walking sticks and quizzing-glasses, cypher badges, even from toys and collars of favored hunting dogs. Catherine the Great's whippet is said to have worn collars to match its mistress's *parures*. The reigns of both Elizabeth and Catherine were a heyday for the lapidary and the jeweler.

Catherine the Great had her Crown of State remodeled by her predecessor's Swiss jeweler, Pauzie, to suit her head as well as her taste: its traditional cleft shape, however, was retained. It is intriguing that a certain diamond hairpiece in the shape of an aigrette, that stands high from the wearer's head, is present time and again in contemporary portraits of the Empress Catherine I, Elizabeth and Catherine herself. A very human touch, perhaps with some special meaning for these ladies. We shall never know.

Enamel, too, enjoyed a rebirth in the eighteenth century. It owed a good deal of its popularity to Catherine, who demonstrated a fondness for it, particularly for the opaque white variety decorated with delicately inlaid thin strips of bronze. Enamel had been in the almost exclusive use of the

Church, the Tsars and the nobility prior to Catherine's reign, when it came into more general use.

Very few of the above mentioned articles ever appear on the commercial markets of the West, other than perhaps a piece of bejeweled embroidery, an occasional item of the white enamel or some jewelry. The story of the development of these art forms leads to the nineteenth century and to production which was more easily available and not too difficult to locate today.

There were three items of intrinsically Russian nature which enjoyed the jewelers' attention: the *bratina,* the *stoulchik salonka* and the *kovsh;* the story of each object is of interest.

First, the *bratina* (*brât* means brother in Russian), the name of which explains its function: it is "the goblet of brotherly love," and its origins, like those of the *kovsh,* are as old as Russia herself. Handleless and circular, the *bratina* was passed from one person to another in the friendship ritual. The complicated and stylized Cyrillic inscriptions that decorate the rim usually declare brotherly sentiments.

The *stoulchik salonka* is a salt container fashioned in the shape of a chair; a cavity in the seat holds the salt. It is a necessary part of the traditional Russian welcoming ceremony at which bread and salt are presented to a guest: the salt chair on such occasions is placed on the concave top of a circular loaf of black bread. An old Russian saying of the people states that: "Without bread, without salt, a meal is but half a meal."

Originally these salt containers were made from bone, ivory, horn, later from base metal, and eventually from gold or silver. They were often embellished with enamels and gems, sometimes with appropriate phrases inscribed on them. By the nineteenth century they had developed into objects of art and all but lost their meaning.

Early in pre-Tartar Russian history, wooden dippers were used for ladling up beverages from a communal cup or bowl. These dippers were called *skopkary.* Gradually they increased in size and became elongated, with an animal or a bird head at one end and a slightly elevated tail protruding from the other for use as a handle. Sometimes *skopkary* had hooks along their sides from which smaller ones were hung. *Skopkary* finally developed into the splendid *kovsh,* which, like the salt chair (though not the *bratina*), lost its purpose and became an *objet d'art,* but in reality an object which retained its usefulness. The latter day *kovsh* was usually decorated with overall shaded *champlevé* enameling: the earlier ones were often undecorated, the simplicity of their graceful lines being sufficient decoration in themselves, however, sometimes an Imperial eagle decorates the nose, and Cyrillic writing the sides.

The salt chair and the *kovsh* in various shapes and sizes are found fairly often on the open markets of the West, but not so the *bratina* or chalice. For purposes of identification, if hallmarks are not present, Russian chalices are always circular in shape.★

During the course of the nineteenth century all the great jewelers and goldsmiths in Russia competed in the production of evermore unusual and beautiful objects. Research into the production of enamelware intensified, as did public interest. The contest was won by a jeweler named Fabergé, but we will come to him shortly.

Enameling is a demanding occupation, as every detail in the preparation of the objects to be fired has to be watched meticulously, for the slightest miscalculation in quantity, quality or in degree of heat in the kilns can lead to disaster. Fusion is the essence of enamel work.

The cloisonné enameling process entails the attachment of tiny compartments to the foundation plaques (the prepared surfaces onto which the enamel is fused); the enamel in liquid form is poured into the compartments—the walls of the compartments separate the different colors. The piece is then heated at about 300°, or the *petit feu* temperature. By the twentieth century a palette of seven tones had been achieved, and the problem of shading had been mastered.

Champlevé enameling entails the excavation of tiny compartments in the

---

★A magnificent collection of seventeenth and eighteenth century Russian chalices may be seen at the Hillwood Museum in Washington, D.C.

foundation plaques, into which the enamel in liquid form is poured, then heated. Careful polishing follows to erase irregularities until the product is as smooth as silk.

Niello work consists of linear designs infilled with black enamel. This should also be as smooth as silk to the touch on completion.

The production of translucent, or *plique à jour* enamel, which is probably the most complicated of all processes, involves the firing of transparent layers of enamel in a *grand feu,* or about 600–800° c. Sometimes several layers of different colors are employed, and *paillons* of gold leaf are often inserted between the layers. The completed article remains translucent, and the colors are spectacular.

Yet other effects are achieved by a technique called *guilloché* which involves the application of a combination of opaque and translucent enamels onto an engraved pattern on a field of gold. The result is much like opaline glass—fire darts beneath the surface.

Jewelry work for the religious community was carried out in monasteries and convents, in the workshops of jewelers and goldsmiths, including privately owned workshops maintained on family estates, such as those of the Sheremetievs at Ostankino and the Youssoupovs at Arkhangelskoye.

The skills required were great. The *riza* was among the greatest challenges and test of imaginative production. Because of the many candles and *lampady* which burn perpetually before the icons in every Russian church, soot, together with the dirt laid down by time, inevitably damaged the paintings. Very little was known about the restoration of icons, and they were often overpainted. Metal covers, called *rizas,* were used to protect icons in as early as the seventeenth century. Before that icons were not shielded but often decorated with a silver (or brass) surround called a *basma,* the patterns on which can sometimes date the century of production. Strips of metal were used to create yet another form of icon cover, an *oklad,* which covered the neutral areas of a depiction as well as the borders. It was only the *riza* that left just the faces, hands and feet exposed to view; on Greek icons, only the faces remained uncovered.

The *riza* grew in importance as time progressed, until by the twentieth century, it often outshone the icon it was intended to protect. Sometimes, in fact, icons were produced specifically for a particular *riza* with only such areas as were exposed to view being painted, the rest of the panel being blank. Such has been the deterioration of iconographic standards, although this was the exception to the rule.

In 1851 a talented Russian goldsmith, Pavel Ovchinnikov, opened a shop in Moscow. His business prospered because the work emanating from his premises was of the highest quality, proof of his technical virtuosity. He also created jewelry, and for his efforts received the Imperial Warrant. In due course he passed his business on to his son, Mikhail, and concentrated his energies in a school for goldsmiths and enamelers which he established. There he trained craftsmen in the mysteries of enameling, resulting in an output of superb artifacts from the workshops. Many of his pupils became master craftsmen in their own right, but unaccountably their names are not as well known as those of the Fabergé establishment, and they do not carry the same magic.

By the nineteenth century many jewelers and goldsmiths were operational among the more important of which, in addition to Ovchinnikov and Fabergé, were: "Lorié, Khlebnikov, Olovyanishnikov, Lioubavin, Sazykov, Morozov and Mishukov, Sbitnev, the British firm Nichols-and-Plincke, Lazarev and Ozersky. Some of them, as well as owning businesses, were workmasters in their own right. It was among such firms that the greatest of them made its impact on the *fin de siècle*. It was that which belonged to Gustave Fabergé, an emigrant from Western Europe, who had opened a small jewelery shop on the Bolshaya Morskaya in St. Petersburg in 1842. In 1870, Peter Carl took over the running of his father's business.

Carl Fabergé was the possessor of a lively imagination, and, more often than not, good taste. The craftsmanship that emanated from his establishment, even the simplest of flatware, was always of the highest quality. He was a perfectionist, and is reputed to have kept a mortar and pestle on his desk into which he ground down items that did not reach the standards of excellence that he had set for his work force. In time Fabergé invented the *objet de vitrine* Easter egg with which he made his name. When Alexander III requested him to fashion one to present to his Empress Maria Fedorovna, the finished product so delighted the Imperial couple that Fabergé was granted the Imperial Warrant.

From that time on he went from one accomplishment to another, and his inventive creativity caught the imagination of the world. He opened a branch of his firm in London, at 48 Dover Street, Piccadilly, then later moved it to 173 New Bond Street, where his fourth son Nicholas was manager with H.C. Bainbridge (who later wrote a book about him). The Russian Empress's sister Queen Alexandra of Great Britain became one of his most valued clients, as did other members of the British Royal family.

The opulence which is so characteristic of Russian art during the second half of the nineteenth and early twentieth centuries was said to be due to the wealth that was concentrated in the hands of a number of aristocratic and merchant families, the richest of all being the Crown. It was a lavish source of artistic patronage which, together with the courts of Western Europe, as well as a few uncrowned American monarchs, encouraged what is now somewhat extravagantly termed "the House of Fabergé." However, in his foreword to H.C. Bainbridge's book, *Peter Carl Fabergé,* Sacheverall Sitwell states:

> And this is another point of interest, the fables of Tsarist extravagance are dissipated in a breath. Even the fabled Imperial Easter Eggs prove to have been no more expensive than a valuable fur coat. The emphasis is upon the craftsmanship more than on the precious stones. Here are no accounts of diamond and emerald tiaras, pearl necklaces and so forth, but a multiplicity of objects ranging from caskets and bonbonnieres to cigarette cases in Karelian birchwood, costing no more than the equivalent of a few pounds. Even the white hollywood boxes in which jewellery pieces of fantasy were sent out were objects of unremitting care.

Opinions were many and varied.

Nicholas II allocated a room for "dear old Fabergé" (as he was wont to call the Master), at Tsarskoye Selo's Alexander Palace, where a large stock of merchandise was kept in reserve for situations when it was required that the Household present a gift.★

Fabergé specialized in delicately detailed small objects such as powder, pill, snuff and other boxes, boxes inset with exquisitely painted portrait miniatures usually surrounded by diamonds, bell-pushes, frames, eggs which split open to reveal icons or which unscrewed to form egg cups, cigarette and card cases, fans, clocks, and, of course, the Easter eggs. One of his ingenious creations was a small golden easel presenting eleven miniature portraits of Alexander III's children, their consorts and their children, all set within a diamond heart. The five-and-one-half inch high nephrite egg which contains the easel is supported by swirls of silver-gilt for its foot, and branches decorate it terminating in rose colored, enamelled, diamond-set pansies. (Collection Dr. Armand Hammer.)

Later Fabergé's interest turned to fashioning small figurines and animals in semi-precious stone, and floral creations. In one such arrangement pearl lilies of the valley tremble on green-gold stems with nephrite leaves in an opaque glass vase. All the work of Fabergé married Russian mineral wealth with colored golds, often in the manner of the eighteenth century *quatre couleur* of the French goldsmiths. Enamels were used with crystals, pearls, pressed flowers, fossils, gems and semi-precious stones. He was capable of transforming ordinary wooden boxes into dramatic and exotic objects with snakes delineated by tiny diamonds, and the clasps were wrought of gold, with rubies, emeralds, sapphires and moonstones in cabochon form. He often drew on ancient Scythian, Byzantine and Russian designs, and also favored neo-Classical swags of flowers, lovers' knots and urns, as well as the eighteenth century affinity for marrying malachite with gilt bronze, and lapis lazuli with silver, the style of decoration that was so greatly favored by Catherine the Great. His fertile imagination

---

★As a child the author's mother had occasion to visit an aunt at her "grace and favor" apartment in the Alexander Palace, where she met Fabergé at tea. Later, she was given permission to accompany him to this stockroom where she was dazzled by the row upon row of enchanting small stone figurines along its shelves. Carl Gustafovich presented her with one of them, a bird with a broken wing. Following emigration and my birth, this little bird's destiny was to help provide for my education.

knew no bounds, and a mystique developed around his personality which has continued to the present day. A coterie of craftsmen gathered round him. (See page 82 for list of craftsmen and their marks.)

These men, and others, helped Fabergé to create an establishment which is considered to be second to no other in the history of applied arts. They elevated him, like Diaghilev, to the position of a cult figure in the arts of pre-Revolutionary Russia.

Several collections of Fabergé's work exist which, from time to time, are presented for public viewing. Her Majesty Queen Elizabeth II displays hers in the Queen's Gallery at Buckingham Palace. In the United States, Christopher Forbes has twelve of the vitrine-type eggs in addition to a considerable number of other pieces, known as the *Forbes Magazine Collection;* it was recently exhibited in New York. Other private collections exist, but are only displayed to the general public when their owners permit.

In June to September 1977, Kenneth Snowman (Chairman of Wartsky, London) mounted a remarkable exhibition, *Fabergé, 1840–1920,* in cooperation with the Victoria and Albert Museum in London. Roy Strong, the museum's director at that time, in his foreword to the museum's catalog, states that:

> For some the art of Fabergé may well seem trivial, a pandering to *fin de siècle* decadence as epitomised by late Victorian and Edwardian England and the last years of Tsarist rule in pre-Revolutionary Russia. Such an attitude is understandable in a more egalitarian age with its dismissive regard toward *objets de luxe.*

He qualifies this by concluding:

> But such a position, if applied consistently to the decorative arts, would rob us of a vast number of its most remarkable creations.

CHAPTER NINE

The Imperial Russian Easter Egg

*T*he egg, like the fish and the anchor (which is a disguise for the cross), is an early Christian symbol, and in nineteenth century Russia, Easter was always celebrated with gifts of eggs. These were fashioned from precious metals, treen, glass, porcelain or a colored hard-boiled hen's egg was an appropriate gift. Traditionally the egg was red signifying happiness and light, in fact, the Resurrection of Christ. The word *krossata* (beauty) is derived from the word *red;* St. Vladimir earned the appellation the Little Red Sun for his introduction of Christianity into Russia. The Red Square in Moscow was so named from the earliest of times, and the Red Corner of a room is where icons are kept.

In ancient times the egg was a symbolic object. It was used in pagan rituals in connection with fertility, and the eating of an egg was considered to protect one from sorcery and enchantment. For this reason in certain areas of Russia any festivities which incorporated eggs into their proceedings were once banned by the medieval all-powerful Orthodox Church. In later times the custom of giving or exchanging eggs at Eastertime became an elaborate ritual when porcelain was invented; by the second quarter of the nineteenth century eggs of great beauty were produced by the various porcelain factories.

Russian eggs can always be distinguished from those made in other countries because they are hollow, with a hole at either end for a looped ribbon to be passed through by which they are suspended beneath an icon.

When true porcelain was first produced in Russia for the Empress Elizabeth Petrovna in 1751 by Dmitri Vinagradov (1720–59), production did not include eggs. The fashion for eggs as objects of art did not become firmly established until the nineteenth century. Very few eggs ever carried any manufactory's identifying mark. Just as icons were seldom signed by their creators, they were painted to glorify the Almighty and not for personal conceit. Jeweled *brelki,* or charm-sized miniature eggs, are usually hallmarked on their suspension loops. Ornamental and miniature eggs were a nineteenth-century manifestation, contemporary with the opulent and fabulous vitrine pieces of Carl Fabergé.

It was the charming custom at Eastertime for men to present their womenfolk with miniature eggs to be worn from the day of the Resurrection for exactly forty days until Ascension Day. They were fixed onto chains worn round the neck, and only round the neck, never on bracelets or as earrings. Men sometimes wore an egg on a watch chain; regimental badges, personal crests or initials were favored for decorating these. People collected eggs from childhood and magnificent necklaces were thus assembled.

Modest wooden eggs were also produced, and their decoration usually consisted of the words *Hristos Voskresse* ("Christ is Risen"), carved or painted ornamentally upon them; sometimes an abbreviation of these words was used: *X.B.* (H.V). The quality of the egg reflected the means of the giver.

Eggs came to be produced with the most diversified and imaginative designs, and in all (portable) sizes and colors. The decoration was mainly of a religious nature, the most popular subject being Christ's Ascension.

Floral designs, too, were painted, with great delicacy and detail. Ethnic art forms were often employed, and love knots, swags of laurel leaves, garlands and symmetric and asymmetric designs but never idyllic scenes, dashing troikas or other secular subjects. Porcelain eggs bearing regimental and naval emblems and those of the Orders of Chivalry, however, were produced, and the ribbons with which they were threaded were of relevant colors; the St. George eggs, for example, carried the black and orange ribbon of that Order.

All the members of Russia's Imperial family were conscientious adherents to the custom of presenting eggs at Eastertime, and porcelain eggs bearing their personal crowned cyphers were manufactured in great abundance. These were destined as gifts, the importance of a specific ocasion, or dignitary, determining the quality of the egg chosen for presentation. Small white eggs which bore a simple, undecorated crowned cipher were made for the armed forces, for factory and field workers and for the general public. During Russia's war years (1914–17) such eggs carried a small red cross on the reverse side to the giver's cyphers, thus dating production. Today, the original *raison d'être* of these eggs is forgotten, and they are collected for their scarcity value and beauty.

Possibly the most elusive of the eggs that carry historic connotations is that given to the last Empress by her children. It was larger than the usual porcelain Easter eggs, and was painted with all manner of mauve flowers—mauve was the Empress's favorite color—violets, pansies, irises, freesias, lilacs. Called *The Childrens' Egg,* it was kept in her mauve boudoir among her icons. Nothing is known as to its whereabouts, and there are no illustrations of it. It is known, however, that many of the Empress's personal belongings were sold to tourists for much needed foreign currency by the early Bolshevik Government. Her sable coats, for example, were sold for £10 each, so this egg might well have suffered a similar fate.

Bejeweled eggs were also produced in sizes larger than the *brelki,* and jewelers entered into heated competition with one another to fashion the finest and most *recherché* of these. Renowned goldsmith Pavel Ovchinnikov led the field for many years particularly with his enamels. He was only surpassed when young Carl Fabergé entered the stage.

The eggs that Fabergé created for the sad, harassed and anxiety-ridden Nicholas and Alexandra were masterpieces of workmanship and imagination, and brought them considerable pleasure. Among the more important eggs that Fabergé produced was the *Tercentenary Egg* (all eggs were given names); much thought went into the design since its purpose was to celebrate the 300-year rule of the Romanov dynasty.

The completed article is constructed of gold covered with opalescent white enamel. The minute cleft Crowns of State, tiny Caps of Monomakh and two-headed eagles are interspered between portrait miniatures of previous Romanov rulers, painted on ivory and set in diamonds positioned around the egg. The whole composition is supported by a fantastic three-winged eagle and stands on a purpurine base. When opened the egg reveals a blue steel globe divided into two sections: the first depicts the Russian Empire as it was in 1613, the second as it had become by 1913. This egg may be viewed today at the Moscow Kremlin.

Some eggs were of quite remarkable beauty and workmanship, eggs such as *A Memory of Azov,* which is carved from a block of solid jasper and decorated with golden waves highlighted with small diamonds. A tiny replica of the *Pamiat Azova* in gold (the ship in which Nicholas II, when Tsarevich, traveled to Japan in 1890, with Prince George of Greece) reposes on a sea of aquamarine.* Another egg is of rock crystal within a fine-mesh net of diamonds; within is an equestrian figure of Alexander III: the metalwork is platinum.

In 1912 Nicholas II presented his mother with the *1812 Egg,* which commemorated Napoleon's invasion of Russia in 1812. Green *guilloché* enamel and a profusion of neo-Classical designs in the Russian style, including the two-headed eagles and military emblems in gold, decorate the egg's casing. It opens to reveal a six-sectioned concertina of miniatures by Vassili Zoiev; the subjects are men in the uniforms of the various

---

*Prince George of Greece was instrumental in thwarting an assassination attempt on the Tsarevich in Japan, for which action Alexander III invested him with the Order of St. Andrew the First-Called.

regiments of which the Empress Dowager was Honorary Colonel, or in Russian parlance, which were "Her Own." They are set in salmon-colored enamel frames with gold borders; her personal crowned cypher in diamonds within circles of green *guilloché* enamel centers the back of each individual frame. As in the case of the *Tercentenary Egg*, the workmaster was Hendrik Wigström.

Although Fabergé's main establishment and workshops were in St. Petersburg, there were branches in Moscow and Odessa, and many of the heavier pieces such as candelabra, *surtout de table, garniture de cheminée,* vases, samovars and *arbouzniki* (watermelon containers) were fashioned there, as were parts for later assembly at other locations. A section of the Moscow workshops was exclusively set aside for the manufacture of eggs.

One further egg should be described here becuase it is one of the most delightful in the Forbes Collection. It was presented by Nicholas II to his Tsaritza in 1895, his first Easter gift to her after their marriage in 1894. Most appropriately, Cupid's diamond-studded arrows point toward a miniature of the Tsar which is set beneath a table diamond. This *Rosebud Egg*, although not as dramatic as the *Madonna Lily*, the *Pelican*, the *1916 Steel Military* or the *1812 Napoleonic Egg*, is certainly the most tender and loving one that he ever gave her.

When the *Rosebud Egg* opens, a life-size rosebud of gold decorated with green and yellow enameling nestles in the velvet-lined interior. The most delicate mechanism provides the surprise which Fabergé was wont to incorporate into much of his work: the rose petals open to reveal a miniature replica of the traditional cleft Russian crown, as well as a small ruby Easter egg; the latter tiny treasures, alas, are lost to posterity. The egg is only two-and-a-half inches long; the gold casing is covered with translucent strawberry-colored enamel and adorned with vertical gold bands set with rose diamonds. The egg is fully hallmarked and dated 1895: it carries the crossed anchors of St. Petersburg production. The workmaster was one of Fabergé's most gifted senior masters, Mikhail Pershin, a Russian.

Other courts placed orders with the firm, as well as wealthy Americans. Christopher Forbes, for example, says that Fabergé made the *Pink Serpant Egg* for the Duchess of Marlborough, née Consuelo Vanderbilt, which is now in his collection. In reply to my query, the present Duke of Marlborough wrote that no record of it exists at Blenheim Palace, and that he believed it to be with his sister, Lady Sarah Rubanis, who resides in California. I have since ascertained, that in 1965, it was purchased by the Forbes Collection for $50,000 at auction.

Queen Alexandra of Britain was another avid collector of Fabergé's work, as was Queen Mary who followed her as Queen Consort. Today their collections repose at Sandringham (a British Royal residence) and were recently exhibited at the Queen's Gallery at Buckingham Palace. Her Majesty's collection is discussed in Kenneth Snowman's book *Carl Fabergé*.

Many further fabulous and fantastic eggs were devised by this gifted artist and his team of workmasters. In their fashioning they included varicolored golds and enamels that were combined with precious and semiprecious stones; tissue-thin slivers of crystal were covered with gossamer nets of diamonds; the *objects de vitrine* pieces often carried flowers on their green gold stems, and even plain wooden eggs and other objects were made to look exotic when golden serpents-of-wisdom slithered across surfaces, spattered with tiny diamonds.

In all fairness to other Russian jewelers and goldsmiths of the day, many of them produced work comparable to Fabergé's in quality, but it was the sustained excellence of Fabergé's imaginative production that placed him head and shoulders above the others.

The collecting of Russian Easter eggs is still possible, both those of glass, porcelain and the *brelki*. The collecting of the splendid *objet de vitrine* ones, however, is beyond most people's means.★

★This chapter, in part, was published in the March 1989 edition of the British publication, *The Antique Collector*.

CHAPTER TEN

The Golden Age of Russian Malachite

*T*he term *Russian Malachite* does not necessarily refer to the stone itself, but rather to its assembly which the Russians perfected. Malachite objects are favored by the collector, but the pieces must be "right," in more ways than one. An explanation of the origins, makeup and use of malachite will make clear the meaning of *right* in this context.

In every country of the world malachite's use has been for decorative purposes. For the collector of Russian art, its story begins in the second quarter of the nineteenth century when the great Demidov Rock was discovered in the Urals. Never before had malachite been found in such quantities or of such beauty.

A workable stone, green in color with shadings ranging from blue-green to almost black, malachite in section has an extremely pretty, intricate design produced by its sinter formation. From the minerological point of view, malachite is a hydrous copper carbonate; it is formed by carbon dioxide-loaded waters passing through copper sulfide and is usually found in its upper layers. This stone was often found in certain areas of Eastern Russia but not all its varieties were suitable for processing. Only the particular malachite in two districts proved to be suitable. These were the Gumishev mine, discovered in 1702, and the more important Mednorudiansk mine, owned by the Demidov princes (San Donato) and discovered in 1835. In 1836 the *Mining Journal* published a sketch of it, together with a detailed description of the black mass which weighed 3,000 *puds* (approximately 250 tons).

At the time of this find there already existed in Russia highly developed techniques for handling decorative stone. The work was principally at Peterhof (today Petrodvoretz) and Ekatirinburg, both manned by artisans of great skill and ability. The Demidov find, however, completely altered the whole concept of the use of malachite. In the second half of the eighteenth century, malachite had been considered a semi-precious stone, and was used mainly for the making of small objects such as earrings, brooches and buttons, tiny vases and small caskets. The Demidov find made new designs possible and paved the way for monumental creations. New techniques for working the stone were perfected and eventually these became known as *Russian Mosaic*.

Three varieties of malachite were primarily used to which the Russians gave names. First, *Miatoi Barkhot* (crushed velvet) which is very beautiful when finished; it produces an almost black play of light on an opalescent surface, but it is very difficult to work on account of its radial structure which, in fact, produces the opalescence. Second, *Lentochnoi* is ribbon-like. Third, *Glaskomi* is spotted and resembles the Karelian birch design: this is the bluish or turquoise variety with curly markings. It is easy to work and is the most rare and valuable.

The construction of malachite articles is unique. Mosaic techniques have been known in Italy for centuries where stonecutting has a great tradition, but, in general, veneering with tiny stone laminae was practiced and only on small surfaces. The Russian malachite technique combines the art of the stonecutters with that of the mosaicist. Because of their thorough familiarity with the stone, the Russians were able to solve the problem of producing large objects. Although the finished objects appear monolithic, they, in fact, consist of thousands of tiny pieces of malachite.

Technically speaking, the application of malachite ornamentation and the creation of malachite articles, unless they were minute, was always a veneering process, similar to that used for any other stone veneer. Where curved or rounded forms were attempted, thicker veneers were used, and the final shaping was made after assembly. This was particularly difficult and required super-human skill and patience. The difficulties lie in the fact that malachite is so fragile that it powders away under the slightest application of pressure. The fixing of the laminae to the outside of a carefully prepared surface, which, in Russia, was predominently slate or copper, was done by a process that gradually heated the base surface of the malachite. A special mastic was applied to the heated base; this green substance was composed of a mixture of pine resin, wax and malachite powder. The object was washed after the application of each and every chip. Green Crocus, a synthetic, abrasive mixture was then used to give it a final polish. The object was then dry-rubbed until it was perfectly smooth and shone like a mirror. These are methods which present-day restorers of chipped and broken malachite objects find difficult to simulate; their efforts always remaining visible to the naked eye upon close inspection.

Many recipes for fixing masses and the Green Crocus are no longer known, and other ancient secrets of processing appear to be lost. The entire art of the working of malachite has been in decline for well over a hundred years.

During the malachite age, in order to assure the supply for the commissions that were sent from palaces, foreign embassies and commercial delegations, as well as domestic consumption, the suppliers of malachite had to obtain permission from the Crown Office for the sale of, and even for the processing of it. This became ever more difficult a situation as the fashion for the stone increased and further orders poured in from abroad. Malachite was sold by the Demidovs for 800 rubles a *pud,* which was a vast sum at that time.

Examples of monolithic workmanship can be seen in the museums, churches and palaces in the Soviet Union today, good examples are the spectacular, soaring columns within the Cathedral of St. Isaac in Leningrad, which de Montferran built in the nineteenth century.

The columns, pilasters and other ornamentation of an entire room at the great Winter Palace on the river Neva (in Leningrad) were designed in 1830 by the same Frenchman; it came to be known as the Malachite Hall. A great many malachite objects, massive tazzas, torchères and candelabra, tabletops and clocks, vast bowls, eggs and balls of solid malachite in various sizes, boxes and caskets, handbells and paperweights, are on display there, and additional items exist in the museum's reserve collection. The objects that are on view at Leningrad's Hermitage Museum today are sufficiently representative to convey an excellent picture of what was once achieved in both large and small malachite pieces, as well as the elegance of the lifestyle that once flourished there.

Malachite in profusion creates a dazzling effect as well as a tremendous elegance. When it is "married" to gilt bronze the results are often breathtakingly lovely. The architect de Montferran and others of the day all loved this intriguing stone and were responsible for its ornamental use in innumerable homes and palaces, as well as public buildings. They carried the malachite-bronze decoration onto frames, bases for busts figures and figurines, onto various orders of architecture, entablatures, pillars and pilasters, cariatides, friezes and particularly onto tabletops. Malachite, in fact, had no rival until 1850–51 when an outstanding minerologist from Peterhof's lapidary workshops, Grigori Perimykin, discovered large deposits of lazurite in the upper reaches of the river Slioudianka in Siberia. This beautiful stone came to parallel malachite in popularity and demand, but it never surpassed it.★

Today malachite arouses the greatest interest and judging by the prices it realizes at auction, collectors are numerous and discerning. Present-day

---

★Lazurite is the blue part of lapis lazuli, which is a complex silicate containing sulfur.

roughly veneered imitations are passed over, and only the real thing reaches substantial figures. Many fakes are circulating in imitation of articles that were fashioned in the Russia of a century ago and more, but even the inexperienced observer can see the difference between the genuine article and a counterfeit. It is not only that the ores used in the imitations are poor in color, texture and pattern but the *essential art of assembly,* so enchanting in the originals, is completely lacking.

Suggestions for collectors, or would-be collectors, of malachite are straightforward. First, naturally, the stone has to be recognized, which is not difficult because of its distinctive coloring. A saunter through any major museum would probably bring one face to face with some examples of it. In the United Kingdom, the Wellington Museum at Apsley House contains some splendid pieces that were presented to the Iron Duke when he visited Russia. Second, quality has to be appreciated. By scouring antique shops and art galleries (not necessarily those that specialize in Russian art), and closely examining each and every piece the eye can be taught to distinguish quality from poor workmanship; it would also teach one to recognize restoration. The malachite base of bronzes are often found to be of modern construction. Their purpose is to add value to an article, and sometimes to trick a prospective buyer into thinking that the item is of Russian origin.

In America there exist many collectors of malachite, and galleries such as *À la Vieille Russie* on Fifth Avenue in New York often possess malachite items among their treaures. Proprietors of such establishments would be delighted to point an interested person in the direction where malachite could be viewed.

CHAPTER ELEVEN

Sculpture

*P*ortrait sculpture in the round of human likenesses was forbidden by the medieval church in Russia, although, as has already been said, an occasional lapse occurred. By the eighteenth century, however, there was a general relaxation of church strictures, and the dormant art form finally came into its own, but predominently in production for the secular world.

Notwithstanding church tradition, the sixteenth century saw some sculpture in churches: heads of John the Baptist, a few renditions of Christ, occasional figures of the Mother of God (as she is always called in Russian parlance,) and, of course, low-relief icons of St. Nicholas of Mojhaisk, the equestrian St. George, and the Mother and her Child. Such artifacts, however, were very often smashed to pieces by fundamentalists, and those that remain are comparatively rare.

Initially the production of sculptures in marble and stone, as well as bronze, depended heavily on foreign sculptors whom Peter the Great brought to Russia to introduce this most important section of the major decorative arts to his subjects. He also imported worked marbles and bronzes of various kinds to act as touchstones, but, although some of them were of considerable merit and vintage, many were simply copies and rough casts of originals. The allegorical figures in the Summer Garden in St. Petersburg, for example, were of such poor quality that they became cause for considerable derision. Funerary statuary, however poor in quality, did not.

Naturally, all the sculptors who arrived in early nineteenth century Russia, most by way of St. Petersburg and its environs, produced busts of the Tsar, his family, and important dignitaries and notables. Count Carlo Rastrelli ("the Elder"), who arrived in 1716, was one such. His bronzes of Peter, of the powerful statesman Prince Menshikov and of many others earned for him the post of Court Sculptor. Possibly his best known work is a large bronze group of the Empress Anna Ioanovna with her small negro page (Russian State Museum, Leningrad). His equestrian bronze of the Tsar, which finally found a resting place opposite Paul I's Michael Castle (Leningrad), is one of his less successful works. He lived out his life in Russia to whose artistic riches he contributed much, including a vast collection of commemorative plaques, and there he found fame and fortune, and died in 1744. His son, Bartolomeo Rastrelli the Younger, the brilliant exponent of "Russian Baroque," became Court Architect and a favorite of Elizabeth Petrovna.

Gradually new men emerged who, after the traditional visits to Italy and France, returned home to produce and inspire a new era of activity in this particular sphere of the arts. They were joined shortly by a veritable galaxy of talent as it emerged from the Academy of Arts following its inauguration in the mid-century. A particularly great talent was that of Shubin.

Fedot Ivanovich Shubin (1740–1805) is considered to have been Russia's greatest sculptor, past or present. His portrait busts in the round are as sound in their geometric coherence as they are soft and sensuous to the eye. His origins were like those of his illustrious friend and contemporary Mikhail Lomonossov (see Chapter Four). They both came from Denisovka near the White Sea. In 1759 when the time came for them to further their talents, Lomonossov went off to Moscow, Shubin to St. Petersburg.

Following the founding of Academy of Arts by the Empress Elizabeth in 1757, her lover, Count Ivan Shuvalov, became its first President. By some ingenious means Shubin obtained an interview with him, and in 1761, through Shuvalov's good offices, he was accepted for tuition at the Academy where he was fortunate to have for his tutor the talented French sculptor Nicholas Gillet (1709–91), who later became the Academy's Director. Shubin was no novice to the plastic arts. It was his proficiency as a bone carver as a child that had persuaded his father to send him to the new capital in the first place.

In 1767 Shubin completed his studies with a gold medal which carried a scholarship for foreign travel, and the Academy sent him to Paris. There he entered the French Academy of Arts, studying under the sculptor Jean Baptiste Pigalle (1714–85), author of the celebrated depiction of the Maréshal de Saxe, and the leader of the French Realists at that time. This tendency immediately appealed to Shubin, and a liking for it remained with him all his days, finally leading to his downfall. Realism is clearly discernable in his work, always true to the subject. It never flattered, and remaned clearcut, definitive and honest. After three years in France, Shubin left for Rome where he spent three additional years at his own expense. As his stipend had run out, he worked on a commission basis.

A great deal of Shubin's work in Italy came his way through his former benefactor Shuvalov, who had made Rome his home after the death of Elizabeth in 1762. Shuvalov knew everyone of any consequence in the city and opened many doors for the young sculptor. He was responsible for his first commission to portray the Demidovs (San Donato), who were in Rome at that time, as well as the Orlov brothers, friends of the new Empress Catherine II. Shubin's work received immediate acclaim and he was made an honorary member of the most ancient Bolognian Academy of Art. In 1774 he returned to Russia as an internationally respected Master.

News of Shubin's successes preceded him, and on his arrival he was presented with a commission to sculpt the Empress and also Potemkin.★ This work was successfully completed and he was created a full member of his own Academy of Arts as a result. In spite of the fact that sculpture was still a comparative novelty to the Russians, as indeed was realistic painting, remarkable beauty of the work brought him adulation and a flood of commissions.

The Russian people called him "the poet of humanity." The porcelain-like fragility of his portraiture placed him squarely in the forefront of his country's plastic arts, but having sculpted an alarmingly, even grotesquely lifelike portrait-bust of Catherine's successor, the unbalanced Emperor Paul, his popularity began to wane. A further blow came in 1801, when his studio was gutted by fire and a great deal of his best work was lost. He died in 1805 in penury, unnoticed and unsung. The coterie of artists that had formed round Shubin, including men of the caliber of Martos and Kozlovsky, prolonged the influence which he had exerted on sculpture in his lifetime, and it continued well into the nineteenth century.

When Catherine the Great decided to erect a monument to her il-lustrious predecessor Peter the Great, for whom she held great respect and admiration, it is said that she was unable to find a sculptor in Russia to suit her needs. This is difficult to comprehend since she had such spectacular talent around her. She had, however, a particular liking for the work of a Frenchman called Étienne-Maurice Falconet (1716–91), and through the efforts of her "Ambassador for the Arts," a Baron Grimm, and his friend, the encyclopedist Diderot, Falconet arrived at Court in 1767. He set to work immediately upon his proposed rendering of the Tsar, having

---

★On inquiring for information from the Victoria and Albert Museum as to what Russian sculpture it possessed (I had heard that they had acquired a Shubin), I received an enigmatic reply stating: "There is a marble bust of Catherine the Great by a Russian sculptor on display in the Jones Collection in Gallery 7." This, of course, is the Shubin.

A superbly dignified marble head of Peter I by Shubin exists in a private collection in Belgium. This masterpiece was once a prized exhibit at the Bowater Gallery, Ltd., in London.

agreed with Catherine on the exact manner of its presentation. It was to be a vast equestrian figure of Peter seated upon a great unruly, rearing horse; Peter's arm was to be flung out in the direction of his beloved West, implying the Tsar's strength in overcoming problems.

But the entire project was filled with difficulties, not the least of which lay in the resentment of the many local sculptors who considered that the work should have been placed in Russian, not foreign hands. Falconet met with unending obstacles, not the least of which was difficulties finding foundries to cast his bronzes. Shuvalov by this time had been replaced by Count Betskoy as President of the Academy of Arts, and he and Falconet never came to an understanding. Finally the Frenchman had had enough, and he left Russia in 1778, his work incomplete—Peter's head had yet to be sculpted. This work fell to his pupil Marthe Callot, who worked tirelessly from various portraits and statues of the Tsar until the work was completed. The full group was finally and satisfactorily cast by Russian foundrymen, and all was ready to be mounted onto the *Grom Kamen (Thunder Rock),* as the huge granite base is called. It had taken men two years to bring its 1,600 tons down from Finland. Chippings of it were used to make commemorative jewelry; Catherine had some, as did her friend, the former Princess of Mecklenburg-Strelitz, and presently the wife of George III of England.

On August 7, 1782, this most imposing and graceful of monuments, which came to symbolize St. Petersburg, was unveiled amid great rejoicing. On its sides were inscribed the words *Petrou ot Ekateriny (To Peter from Catherine).* Miniatures of it were made in bronze, wood, precious and semi-precious stones, in gold and in silver, and these are still found, if with some difficulty, the world over today. The poet Alexandre Pushkin was moved to write a poem about the sculpture which has become a classic of the Russian language; it was translated into English by Sir Charles Johnson. *(The Bronze Horseman)*

By the end of Catherine's reign (in 1896), the Rococo style, which she had preferred to Elizabeth's Baroque because she considered it too heavy and overpowering, had been replaced by the linear neo-Classicism that was sweeping Europe. The rocaille style was replaced by the oak leaf; garlands of bronze wound their way through the short reign of Paul I and into that of his son Alexander (1801–25). But, by the 1830s, neo-Classicism was dead.

Around the years of the Patriotic War (1812) portraits and sculptures of the Tsar, his generals and war heroes were in great demand, and portrait busts of military leaders such as Suvorov, Barclay de Tolly, Bagration and Kutuzov were received with enthusiasm by the public. Lofty patriotism was the spur, and any aesthetic that was connected with the war effort was carried through into the post war years. Architecture, of course, had to concentrate on reconstruction and repairs of the damage caused by Napoleon's rampages, especially in Moscow, and other than the work in St. Petersburg of the architect Carlo Rossi (1779–1849), very little new decorative construction in the manner of the eighteenth century took place—it was gone forever, never to return. But sculpture continued to flourish, and new and exciting exponents joined the older corps of men at work in this particular industry.

Of the older men Ivan Prokofiev (1758–1828) produced four hundred sculptures of merit and versatility, including the biblical *Bronze Serpent* that decorates the Kazan Cathedral; Mikhail Kozlovsky (1735–1802) worked in bronze, marble and gypsum, and specialized in decorative figures from mythology; Feodossi Shchedrin (1751–1825) was a master of the nude, an example being the *Bathing Venus* (marble). Fedor Gordeiev (1744–1810), son of a palace cowherd, had talent that was recognized and he was sent to Paris for study; his best known work is *Prometheus*. Ivan Martos (1754–1835) was among the greater of the neo-Classicists and the producer of the vast bronze group of *Minin and Pojharsky;* he worked closely with the architect Quarenghi, and later collaborated with Carlo Rossi on many projects in St. Petersburg. Among his pupils was the talented Ivan Halberg (or Galberg, 1789–1839), who specialized in portrait sculpture; his seated bronze figure of Catherine the Great was warmly received, and he was created Architect to H.I.M.'s Cabinet (Crown Office).★

★Halberg also sculpted a miniature version of this model of the Empress. It graced the Austrian Embassy in St. Petersburg for many decades. It also graced the author's former gallery for several years, from where it continued on its way.

Among the new generation of sculptors were men such as Alexander Terebeniev (1814–59), the son of the great satirical artist of the 1812, Ivan. He was responsible for the ten vast granite Atlantes that support the lintels of the New Hermitage. (Decorative sculpture was always popular in Russia and the fashion for it continued well into the nineteenth century.) Petr Ivanovich Klodt (a Russified Baltic baron, 1805–67), was an outstanding craftsman and believed to have been Russia's first animal sculptor of consequence. Among his better known works is the statue of the fabulist Krylov that stands in the Summer Garden, the oldest of St. Petersburg's parks. He is also recognized for the splendid horses with their naked handlers that decorate the four corners of the Anichkov Bridge (St. Petersburg). The four groups displeased Nicholas I in whose reign they were created and set in place, causing him to write a remarkably course couplet about them suggesting that the sculptor should be found and given a good hiding; the reason for his displeasure is not clear, for the groups are perfect in proportions and detail. All of Klodt's presentation of the animal world, in fact, may be safely compared with that of such men as Barye and Mêne.

The work of Count Fedor Tolstoy (1783–1873), a pupil of I. P. Prokofiev at the Academy, encompassed that of painter, sculptor, engraver and medallist—he was considered to be the greatest Classicist of the period. He was the gentle poet of the arts, a delicate stylist and the last of the Romantics. A lover of the past, he entertained a devotion for early Greece, and he interpreted Hellenism into Slavophilism. He romanticized women, and painted and sculpted them with small heads, tight curls and large eyes. He sculpted caryatids, and ladies draped languidly across Grecian urns staring enigmatically into the middle distance. His paintings were more realistic in style, among his better known was *The Family Portrait;* interiors were his forte.

In the same way as Rastrelli the Elder produced numerous and diversified coins and medallions, so too did Tolstoy. He worked for many years as a medallion maker and designer at the Hermitage where he was able to imbue his love for Classicism well into the mid century. When Realism finally dismissed the Classicist, Tolstoy turned ever more often to his painting at which he worked until the end of his long and industrious life.

In the latter half of the nineteenth century, workmanship matured, and although those years did not produce the enormous talents that the first half had, some excellent work was executed. With the coming of Slavophilism and the Russian Style, problems lurked for the sculptors because sculpture was alien to medieval Russian fashion, although wood carving, of course, was not. Portrait sculpture, however, retained its popularity.

The most outstanding of the *fin de siècle's* artists was the self-taught Prince Pavel Petrovich Troubetskoy (1866–1938). He is sometimes called a Symbolist artist, no doubt because his work was often executed in an exaggerated, exotic manner (e.g., *Mephistophilese*). But he also produced bronzes in a purely neo-Academic fashion, that is, portraits such as his well-known head of his friend Count Lev Tolstoy (1899), and the posthumous Alexander III (1909). Both were works to which a touch of genius was added, but were never unrecognizable depictions of ideas or fragmentation in the manner of the Symbolists.

Troubetskoy was born in Russia but educated in Milan, where he received some tuition from Bazarro. In Russia he taught at the Moscow School of Painting, Sculpture and Architecture, where one of his pupils was Nathalia Goncharova. With the coming of the Russian Revolution he returned to Italy and worked extensively. He died there immediately before the Second World War in 1938. His work is often found on the Western European markets, but, collectors, beware, numerous modern castings exist, if in limited editions.

The sculpture that was produced in the years preceding the Revolution of 1917 (excluding the work of the Constructivists, Cubists, Suprematists and others) was excellent, but not great. Among the better known sculptors who worked in the neo-Academic style was Mark Antakolsky (1843–1902), whose work was faultless in design and workmanship but of small imagination. Renditions of Peter the Great, Tarakanova, Ivan the Terrible, as well as an uncanonical yet forceful head of Christ, were among his finer works.

There were two great exponents of genre, Grachov and Eugène Lanceré, Alexandre Benois's nephew. They both specialized in delightful groups of peasants, horses and other animals, huntsmen and cossacks— they both produced delightful versions of *The Cossack's Farewell to His Girl*. The essentially Russian element in their work continues to enchant the West today; though prices for it have soared, they do not appear to have damped the collectors' ardor for their acquisition.

The production of miniature and small, portable bronzes, particularly for setting onto rhodonite, lapis lazuli, malachite and marble bases, was prolific in pre-revolutionary Russia. The pieces were exported in great numbers, and such pieces are frequently met with on Western markets. Also, be advised that modern recasts of Russian bronzes are made, often roughly and in spelter, but because Russian foundry marks are in evidence on these castings, they are incorrectly attributed to Russian workmanship.

Look for true patina (the incrustation on bronze that is caused by oxidation, usually brown or green in color), and for sharp, clearcut delineation on an article to ensure that you are handling an original work of art.

CHAPTER TWELVE

Woodwork

*A*ncient Rus was known to its neighbors as the land of the great forests, so wood held a special place in the arts and architecture of the country. The various legends in connection with wood nymphs and forest demons emanating from Rus were accepted with a certain awe by her neighbors. Russian chroniclers tell of many heavily populated towns already existing in the ninth century, with houses, palaces and kremlins with their bulwarks, ramparts and fortresses built of wood.

The ax, as can be imagined, played a significant role in the life of the people, together with the plane, the hammer and the knife—these were the only tools known for both practical and decorative work. The saw made its appearance during the sixteenth century, but it was a luxury and only available for use in the more important locations. Every peasant hut, or *izba,* and house which possessed an ax had a carved likeness fixed above the front door. In the case of fire in the community, it was clear for all to see where there was an ax available for use.

The story of Russian architecture will not be discussed in this book, but its varied decorative style will be since they were often translated in reduced form to miniature buildings, including replicas of specific churches and children's toys. All ethnic art displays its national theme and decorative principles. This was particularly true of Russian carpentry, which was one of the most important forms of folk production.

"Prepare your cart in winter, your sleigh in summer" is a wise old peasant saying, which peasant industry revolved around. Another saying, however, that "Work is for summer, sleep for winter," was not quite accurate. It implies that due to the ferocious Russian winters making work out-of-doors impossible, sleep prevailed. In truth, a veritable hive of industry usually developed in the villages, not only to while away the time, but to augment meager incomes. Furniture, children's cots and toys, *kvas* and ordinary jugs, *skopkary* and *sudny* (broad and boat-shaped containers or dippers), salt chairs, bowls, plates and spoons, distaves, bodkins and spindles were all created in village industry and subject to decoration. Elaborately carved wooden implements called *naboiki* were made for stamping designs onto textiles, and charming, often fantastic, patterns were incised on gingerbread molds. And, of course, the *douga* (shaft bow) and often the back-panels of sledges were carved—Sirin and Alconist motifs were favored to ward off ill fortune during journeys.

All the above-mentioned artifacts are highly collectible and can be quite easily located in antiques markets, and out-of-the-way shops. Auction sales are lucrative hunting grounds for such goods which are inexpensive, and appear to have been brought out of Russia through the years in considerable profusion. Great care should be taken, however, not to confuse them with Scandinavian products, for many items such as *sudny,* bowls and *larzy* (caskets) are very similar and all but impossible to distinguish one from the other at times.

Wooden children's toys have existed from time immemorial, and their styles, naturally, relate to a natural environment. Records exist of wooden toys at archeological digs, and the earliest written documentation of these dates from the ninth century; the more extensive records date from later times. It is known that in 1636 the Court purchased a toy wooden cart and horse from the workshops of the St. Sergius's Monastery of the Holy

Trinity near Moscow, the seat of the Russian Patriarchate. In 1721, Catherine I bought some wooden animals, vessels and soldiers for her children from the same monks.★

The carving of toys and other small items were an important source of additional revenue for monasteries, which were the centers for such production in medieval times. The inexplicable charm of rural production, its simplicity, sincerity and a certain intensity, very often holds its own with the most sophisticated urban production, and this may well be the reason why the Imperial and other porcelain factories very often took carved dolls and the like as models for their creations; orders, in fact, were placed with carpenters for this specific purpose.

One such instance had quite amusing consequences: a certain woodcarver once produced a derogatory figurine of a monk carrying a bale of straw, which, on close inspection, revealed a girl hidden in it. The matter was brought to the attention of Alexander I, whereupon a edict was proclaimed forbidding its production and possession. Later, this figurine was produced in porcelain, and "the Impious Doll" became fairly commonplace; at the time of its initial production it caused a considerable furor.

The rendition of people in specific walks of life was a favorite entertain-

---

★Among the more exciting productions which Russian carpenters and decorator-carvers combined to create was a wooden palace for the Tsar Alexis Mikhailovich. It was called Kolomenskoye, and its foundations were those of a much earlier construction from the days of the fourteenth-century Great Prince Ivan Kalita. Work on it was commenced by an army of serf craftsmen in 1667 and it took about two years to build. The size was vast, and it was a great jumble of structures that were joined to one another by innumerable galleries and corridors. It sported *kokoshnik*-shaped gables, windows, turrets and entrances. The palace fell into disuse by the eighteenth century and became a fire hazard; in 1767 Catherine the Great ordered it demolished, but not before a miniature model of it had been fashioned for her, which is now in a museum. Reproductions of this model are in themselves works of art, but these are few and far between. The author has seen only one in all her years of working in the Russian arts.

The carving of miniature structures enjoyed widespread popularity in Russia. Children's toys very often consisted of shaped bricks which, on assembly, formed such edifices as the Kremlin, churches, palaces and various well known buildings. Jigsaw puzzles, however, were not so commonplace.

ment of the carvers. Fat monks, fops, vain gentlewomen and dandified officers, over-prosperous burghers—all such people whom the peasant carvers saw as "the idle rich"—suffered for the sake of derision, mostly good humored, but not always so. The 1905 post Russo-Japanese War civil disturbances, that are known as the First Revolution, saw a small vitriolic carving come into being. The name of its creator is not known. It depicted three policemen supporting a throne shaped like a hideous demon, on which sits an intoxicated figure of Nicholas II with a bottle in one hand and a crucifix in the other. The fact that this piece came to be mass-produced in porcelain and at considerable expense indicates, yet again, that the revolutionary movement was financially underwritten from somewhere. But it is the earlier production that concerns us here.

Among the ancient toys which the carvers of old were fond of producing was a doll called Matrioshka, whom Soviet scholars consider to have been a version of the Golden Goddess Jumala (mentioned in the Introduction) since her origins were in Viatka, in the foothills of the Urals. Noncanonical and untraditional carved statutes of the lifelike Madonna also sometimes appeared in those regions which were a disguise for Jumala, as were the sets of dolls which unscrew to reveal another and then another. This deity's cult remains a mystery of this day, wrapped as it is in the mists of a Siberian enigma.

There was an age-old predilection to use animalia for decorative purposes, often in the round, especially the Firebird, cocks and bears. Further subjects were Obida, the bird with a girl's face and wings spread wide, as well as the wolf—they both symbolized evil. Obida should not be confused with Sirin and Alconist who represented good. The other popular subjects for artistic exploitation were the Rousalka (the mermaid or water sprite) and the Bogatyr Ilya Mourametz (a heroic knight of ancient legend), as well as the geometrically arranged flowers and scrolls that were carried out in intricate and characteristic designs. No village existed without striking examples of these national art forms in strong evidence. The various carved bands of open tracery which decorated medieval, even the latter day *izbas* exteriors—the eaves, gables, porticoes, windows and their shutters—were all subjects for the carpenters' expertise, and some of the work that was carried out elevated this minor art to levels of true excellence. It is this form of decoration, which is often painted in bright colors, that identifies an article as being of Russian production when it is located outside its country of origin.

More sophisticated skills, however, were required for the production of furniture for the upper strata of society and for palaces. The favored wood for this work was that of a small gnarled tree from the northern tundras. It is called Karelian birch, and its name became exclusively synonymous with Russian furniture. It is a delightful wood with a range of color varying from pale cream to that of rich honey, but it is never brown. It carries a rich pattern of brown and black swirls and dots due to its stunted growth in the deep Karelian wastes near the White Sea. In its own way, the finished polished product came to represent one of the most recherché mediums in Russian decorative arts. Small objects such as boxes, taper holders, playing card and stamp containers, bowls and book stands were often fashioned from it. Occasionally these are found on Western markets; larger pieces such as furniture even less often.

Bark scrolls, often decorated with colored designs, were used for wall paper as well as for *lapti* (peasants' summer shoes). *Polâty,* or benches that were fixed high up above the warmth of stoves in peasant homes, were also often carved; beds, as such, were not in general use until the seventeenth century. The stove was the center of life in every *izba,* and *spâtz na petchki* (to sleep on the stove) is an age-old peasant epithet—the intimation being that he who does so is lazy. Stoves were made of iron; in wealthier homes, however, more often than not they were tiled.

Among the more important subjects for the carpenters and carvers was the *iconostasis,* to which several references have already been made. This is the screen that separates the sanctuary from the nave of a church, with a space called a *kliras* acts as a no-man's land between the two. The *iconostasis* has a tradition governing the manner in which icons are afixed or painted on it on the congregation's side of the structure, which is punctured with three doors for specific entry into the sanctuary. The central doors are called Tsar Gates (never "Royal Doors" since no "royal" title existed in Russia; Greek gates, of course, may be called Royal Doors). These are used by officiating clergy, the two side ones by others. The structure itself is always made of wood, and this is sometimes carved. With the coming of the seventeenth and eighteenth centuries, Baroque and Rococo styles of decoration transferred from secular buildings to affect church decoration. Carvers' efforts to beautify the *iconostasis* with garlands of flowers, fruit and vegetable designs, fluting, frieze and other fretwork very often overwhelmed the icons. Figures of the Holy Family or of the saints, however, are never included in the work.

The *iconostasis,* since it is in situ, cannot be collected, but the icons that decorate its various tiers can be, and these are often found among the goods smuggled out of the Soviet Union today, as are the Tsar Gates. So, too, are the miniature *iconostasis,* which are copies of the originals. These are formed of fifteen panels, with the fourteen side sections folding in upon the central one which contains a painted version of the Tsar Gates. They were used to accompany large groups of people on long journeys, by clergy for various offices that were undertaken outside churches, and at Drumhead Parades. These are eminently collectible and several passed through my gallery. When I found them they were usually in pieces due to the wear and tear of their function. Restoring them to their former beauty always gave me particular satisfaction.

Another essentially Russian form of production were wooden objects usually painted in bright colors—red, black and gold—with a final coating of thick and shiny varnish. Children's furniture was often produced in this style, as well as *sudny,* small barrels and spoons, *kovshes,* etc., all of which are frequently found in the West. These artifacts are useful, colorful and quite charming, a particular variety of the folk arts that grew into a successful export industry, both before and after the Revolution.

Village communities, monasteries and far-flung hermitages all worked in this highly developed, if somewhat static, national art form, and in the northern regions on the carving of bones, walrus tusks, deer antlers and wolf teeth. The treen arts live on in the Soviet Union today, even if the laborious handwork of yore has now been replaced to a certain extent by modern technology.

CHAPTER THIRTEEN

Miscellany

Embroidery and Fashion

A s wood carving in Russia was influenced by ancient styles and motifs, so too was embroidery. Fine cross-stitching in bright colors (usually red, blue, yellow and black) was the most favored among the folk styles, with lions, peacocks, birds and bears, cocks and geometric patterns, and, of course, the Sirin and Alconist designs forever retaining favor. This art form divides into two distinct categories: the ecclesiastical and secular.

The demands of the Church for the needlewomen's skills were vast, and although a great deal of the work was done in convents and, to a certain extent, in monasteries, there were ateliers outside secluded walls that also specialized in such matters; peasant women, too, undertook commissions, and some of their work often took the form of votive offerings. Priests' vestments always needed repair or renewal, as did altar cloths, *analoi* and other table covers, *paleny, nabedreniki,* and the *Plashchennitza* itself. There were certain articles that required more refined, specialized abilities which were undertaken by the various schools of embroidery, or, as has been said, by convents, such as the Novadevichy, near Moscow, renowned for exceptional work.

Embroidery plays a more important role in Russian churches than it does in the West, excluding, of course, some Roman Catholic ones. This is because Orthodox ritual (which has not changed in its thousand years of existence in Russia,) is elaborate and requires supportive adjuncts to its procedures. The embellishment and agrandissement of churches was generally accepted as being necessary for the glorification of the Almighty; in the same manner a sumptuous spectacle was expected of the clergy and was traditional even in the smallest and humblest of village churches.

Among the more important of Orthodoxy's sacramental objects is the *Plashchennitza* to which several references have already been made. Standing midway between a liturgical adjunct and an icon, it represents the moment in the Christian story which took place between the Taking down from the Cross and the Entombment. Its place of rest is within the sanctuary beyond the iconostasis, from where it is brought out on Good Fridays, and is returned with similar solemnity before the midnight Resurrection service on the Saturday. The *Plashchennitza* consists of a rectangular cloth upon which the dead body of Christ is shown surrounded by those who mourn Him. His mother is usually standing above Him or at His feet, and angels hover meaningfully, indicating the presence of heavenly power and grace. At the four corners are small depictions of the Evangelists, or their symbols, to indicate that His word has reached the four corners of the earth.

The *Plashchennitza* is heavily embroidered, usually in gold satin stitching, but the faces and hands of the mourners, as well as Christ's body, are painted iconographically. The embroidery was done by women, the exposed areas of the faces, hands and Jesus's body were painted by (consecrated) men since, until the present century, women were not permitted to "write" icons. To do so continues to be frowned on by fundamentalists.★ In the seventeenth century there was a general relaxation in stylistic icon tradition, and, as in the painting of icons, the style of religious embroidery became softer and began to lose its inherent Slavonic individuality.

Secular embroidery and other decoration of textiles, unrestrained as it was by the Church's canonic strictures, was a blossoming art, as was lace making and other related industries. Village industry, of course, was governed by seasonal rigors in exactly the same way as wood carving, icon painting, the coloring of the *lubok* (to which we will come shortly) were affected. The weaving of textiles, sewing and embroidery was the women's primary industry in winter, and although many of the items that were produced were simple in design, their workmanship was often of the highest and most refined caliber. Many highly illustrated books have been written on this subject, yet the general public conception remains that the work was primitive and of no particular interest; in some cases, of course, this was so.

The main subjects of production were: bed linens, aprons and table-linen, curtains, garments—the traditional high-necked and embroidered mens' shirts and womens' *saraphans*—and, of course, towels. Towels, in Russia, were an important item of production, for in addition to their obvious use, they served as adjuncts to religious worship. They were used to drape across the tops of icons, to present to churches as votive offerings, to be held at the Communion Cup in case of spillage, and across the hands holding the bread and salt at welcoming ceremonies. They were draped over mirrors when death occurred in a home. An ancient custom that is seldom observed now, it was done to prevent a new-born soul from being frightened when it did not see its reflection in passing. Such towels

---

★On a personal level, when I was working at my gallery, I bought, restored and sold icons. Being Orthodox, I was criticized by many people because it was considered sacrilegious to commercialize iconography, but I looked upon my work as the salvation of panels with woodworm and flaking paint. In the end, I was forced to approach the Russian Orthodox Church, from which I received official dispensation, indeed encouragement, to continue, which stilled many tongues.

were always of a considerable length, and the embroidery was at either end. The intricate method for this embroidery was the *dvoukhstaronny shov,* a method of simultaneous stitching which embroidered both sides of a given strip of textile.

Another item that enjoyed particular attention from needlewomen was the *kokoshnik,* a head dress consisting of a band that held a stiffened and shaped canvas form; it was customary for such forms to indicate the districts from which their wearers came. *Kokoshniks* were tall, squat, spiked oval or heartshaped, encrusted with jewels or beads, or heavily embroidered; the quality bespoke the wearer's means and social standing because women from all stratas of society wore them, including the Empresses. Sometimes a veil, or *fatta,* floated down the back, and pearls, particularly river pearls which are abundant in northern rivers, or simply beads, hung to either side of a wearer's face and along the forehead. The ethnic *kokoshnik* in miniature replaced the date stamp on Russian gold and silver from the year 1896.

The main centers for sewing and embroidery by peasant women outside their homes were *terims,* women's quarters in the houses or palaces of nobles—not be confused with harems! There, under the watchful eyes of housekeepers, or the mistress of the house herself, the villagers toiled at the weaving of textiles, lace-making and embroidery, as well as at the more mundane sewing and darning. The printing of decorative designs onto textiles was done in special areas of these quarters. The *naboinik* method was popular, and consisted of pressure being exerted from small wooden blocks which had been carved with designs and inked with vegetable dyes. The *naboika* patterns are of the greatest interest because some of the designs are known to have originated in the twelfth century. (The literal translation of the word *naboika* is "to beat on.")

Fashion changed very little before the reign of Peter the Great, at which time he introduced a total Westernization to the ruling, urban and merchant classes, but only insisted for peasants to shave their beards. Those who did not were fined.

Basically, the peasant clothing consisted of the traditional *kaftan* for men, which was worn over a belted, high necked shirt, and the sleeveless *saraphan* for women; the *paneva,* which was a dirndl-type skirt, was worn for work with a blouse and apron. The men's very wide trousers, *sharovary,* were tucked into heel-less felt or leather *valenki,* which women also wore in winter. As has been mentioned, *lapti,* or shoes that were plaited from thongs made from the inner bark of lime trees, or simply from straw, were fashioned for everyday summer wear. There was a charming custom for a *lapot* to be hung in chicken coops with a stone in it. This indicated to the hens that it was far better for them to lay their eggs at home.

The nobles' traditional garb was simply an elaboration of the peasants' clothing, but in medieval times overlong sleeves were worn to indicate a person's non-laboring role in life. Boots of often red *saphian* leather replaced the peasants' *valenki* and *lapti,* and men's hats consisted of cone shapes over which circlets of wolf, fox, sable, or other furs were lowered. The women's *kokoshniks* have already been described, but smaller and plainer ones were made for everyday wear. The *saraphan,* too, was cut on the same lines as those worn by peasants, only materials were richer. In cold weather short, highly embroidered, fur-lined jackets called *shoushouns* were worn indoors, and full length ones out-of-doors. The quality of the fabrics and decoration were consistent with the means of the wearers.

Civilian clothes reflected those of the army, and *kaftan* lengths rose and fell by its dictates, and went out of fashion when Peter the Great initiated his reforms and innovations. Khaki was adopted for wear during the Russo-Japanese War of 1904–5. Pre-revolutionary Russian uniforms, and other militaria, are collected avidly today.

From the eighteenth century on, Russian fashion progressed in exactly the same way as in the rest of Europe. In the multi-national regions of non-European Russia, fashion remained true to the traditions of its ethnic heritage, in some areas, to this day.

Collectors find it comparatively easy to find various Russian embroideries, individual items such as *lapti, kokoshniks,* even religious desiderata—though not embroidered icons, as such, for they were seldom produced in Russia—but complete ensembles are never found, not even in museums. It is only by visiting the Soviet Union that such things may be viewed in abundance, as Jackie Onassis found when she was preparing her book on the subject of Russian dress, *In the Russian Style.*

In October of 1967 until January of 1968 a magnificent exhibition was mounted at the Grand Palais in Paris, *L'Art Russe des Sythes à nos Jours,* but other than an awesome kaftan of colossal size that had once adorned the frame of Peter the Great, and six other articles of clothing, there was little else. Other exhibitions were held at the Barbican Centre in London recently, and another at New York's Metropolitan Museum which presented Russian dress.

Carpets

The carpet industry was never particularly successful in the Russian Empire, the domestic market being too close to Persia, Turkey and the Caucasus, which for many centuries have monopolized the market for the commodity. This is not to say that a lively carpet making industry did not exist within the Russian Empire. Many regions produced carpets, small rugs, wall hangings, table covers, mats and so forth. Bukhara, now in the Uzbek S.S.R., possessed an active industry that specialized in velvet and silk creations of a superb quality and beauty. And so too did the Tartars who lived in small villages to the east of the Urals, and produced a practical type of carpet from wool that contained very little aesthetic attraction.

Dubova Posad in the Saratov province, Kursk, Khersen and Poltava, Bessarabia and Tiumen Okroug in Siberia's Tobolsk province, and Podolk are regions where carpet making was an established industry. Around 1800, the Yusoupov family brought carpet workers from Poltava to Rakitinoye, but the venture made no profit and was closed in 1831.

Apart from regions such as Bukhara, few areas produced carpets of particular quality or beauty; there appeared to be a lack of overall imagination and inventiveness with regard to decoration. The Aubusson pattern was copied time and again and the further east a location of production lay, the less imaginative the work appeared to become. Disproportionately large animal and bird motifs were great favorites, as well as garlands of flowers or small, impish figures on the borders. The lack of traditional designs led to delightful incongruities, such as bottles and labels copied with religious attention to detail, including the labels' lettering. It was in Asiatic, not European Russia, where carpet making predominated.

The arrival in 1717 of French weavers and instructors for the making of Gobelin-type tapestries heralded one-and-a-half centuries of disappointment. Tapestry work never found favor in Russia. Even the brilliant and powerful French architect under whose protection they had come to Russia, Jean Baptiste Alexandre Le Blond, had been unable to titillate Russian tastes when he introduced tapestries into the interior decoration of palaces and for other commissions. As the industry gradually disintegrated, the manufactories became rug making concerns. By the mid-nineteenth century, other than a few privately owned factories, the center of the industry, the Ekatrinkhof looms, ceased to produce.

An intriguing footnote to the story of the Russian carpet is that in 1949 a carpet was discovered in a Scythian *kurgan*. It was unearthed at Pazyryk in the Altai mountain range, and dates from 500 B.C.

Russian Ivory

Walrus tusk, or Russian ivory carving ranked with the finest *oeuvres* of West European production during the early centuries of known civilization. Northern *kurgans* have exposed pre-Tartar era bonework of a surprisigly high quality and in an excellent state of preservation. Ivory figures of deities and of animals, the heads of birds—in particular profusion, of owls and eagles—jewelry, knife handles and countless other objects have been unearthed. In 1649, Tsar Alexei Mikhailovich decreed bonework to be a state monopoly, and bone carvers were brought from the northern provinces and other areas to the Armory Palace art workshops in Moscow.

Non-canonic icons in bas relief were worked in bone and were often decorated with gold or silver foil, mother of pearl and/or precious or semi-precious stones, sometimes simply with bits of glass. Such icons pleased foreigners if not the fundamentalists, and they were presented as gifts to dignitaries and visitors of note. Bone carvers were also employed on items for personal adornment, as well as on portraiture; an interesting collection of bone carvings exists of forty-nine rulers of the Russian territories from the time of Rurik. They were carved by the country's greatest sculptor Fedot Shubin. He also carved in bone a portrait of his friend, the scientist Lomonossov (of whom mention has been made in the chapter on glass).

With the coming of the nineteenth century, bone carving came to be mass produced, and geographic areas specialized in specific kinds of production. Goblets, caskets and chess sets, models of deer teams and dashing troikas, jewelry, combs, icons and crosses, and many diversified and interesting objects began to appear on the urban markets. The charm and naivité of the earlier pieces, however, were seldom recaptured, even though workmanship grew ever more refined and acceptable to a developing, and progressively ever more sophisticated society.

Ceramics

The Russian ceramic industry is said to have originated in the seventh century under Byzantine influence, long before the Christianization of Rus in 988 A.D. Its development proceeded uneventfully until the appearance of the Golden Horde, at which time there was total disruption in the country's development.

A Tartar people from the country to the north of China rose suddenly to prominence in the world's affairs, and achieved such a series of conquests as has no parallel in history—these were the Mongols.

Such were the words of British writer H.G. Wells. His *Short History of the World* provides considerable detail on the subject of the Tartar-Mongol conquests and makes for intriguing reading.

Once they were consolidated, the Mongols, to whom the Tartars were subservient and who recognized only the Great Khan as sole ruler, proceded to subject the Russians to unimaginable horrors, forcing most industries during the initial years of the conquest to go underground. When they gradually began to emerge, many of them had to start from the beginning.

So it was with ceramics. The *korchaga,* a pitcher-type vessel for carrying liquids, had reached some sophistication in form and design in the pre-Tartar era; examples fashioned in the later thirteenth century are roughly made and purely utiliarian. By the end of the fourteenth century, however, there was a weakening in the Tartar yoke, and all industry began to revive, including that of the ceramics. The crude brown pots gave way to more inventive, imaginative designs.

The various clays that were found in different regions influenced the colorings that emerged from the kilns; the whiter of the clays such as Gzhel produced were processed for the more prestigious production. Old designs revived and vessels were covered with a thin white slip which gave them life. Gradually colored ceramics were perfected which emerged from the kilns undamaged and in perfect shape for their surfaces to be covered with diversified and complicated regional designs drawn from traditional folk motifs, and quite often from nature. A dark gray, near black, color was achieved by introducing soot into a product when the kiln was still heated, but at a low temperature. Strangely, the color became very popular, and has retained favor into the present day. Black ceramics were highly prized in Georgia, and the various means for achieving fine objects are now being researched by the leading Soviet ceramist Revaz Yashvilli; many of the ancient methods have fallen into disuse in recent years.

The production of ceramics progressed in Russia in exactly the same way as it did in the rest of Europe, with national idiosyncracies and preferences influencing its development from region to region. Specific articles were invented for particular uses, i.e., the *kvasnik,* the shape of which proclaimed that its contents was *kvas* (a delicious cider-type beverage made from fermented barley and beetroot); the *rukomoi,* a jug with a large opening for the filling of it, and one or two round spouts for pouring, which was used for the washing hands before meals—tradition indicated that it was unlucky to do so from a bowl. By the end of the seventeenth century, the center of ceramic production and distribution was a Moscow *sloboda* (or suburb), which was replaced in the eighteenth century by Gzhel.

Gzhel and its surrounding villages, an area where some of the country's best clay was located, had been in the possession of the Crown. It was the center for pottery and ceramics first mentioned in documents by Moscow's Great Prince Ivan Kalita ("Moneybags") in the fourteenth century. In the seventeenth century it came to sudden prominence partially because Tsar Alexei Mikhailovich ordered Gzhel clay to be used exclusively by certain Moscow potters. Documentation exists that glazed majolica was sold in Moscow in the late seventeenth century, and that later in the eighteenth century Gzhel became its center of production. Majolica, however, was never in special demand in Russia, although jugs, plates and chargers were fashioned from this low-fired, tin-glazed pottery and usually used for decorative purposes by the less-well-to-do citizens.

In 1801 a German named Carl Otto began producing porcelain at Gzhel, and slightly later a local peasant Pavel Kulikov began production in a nearby village named Volodino. It was near Gzhel that porcelain is claimed to have been discovered in 1747 by a Moscow merchant named Ivan Grebenshcikov, but the story is said to have been hushed up by Baron Tcherkassov, as mentioned earlier. Gzhel, in fact, was a hive of exciting industry, although its porcelain factories were not among the greatest ones in Russia.

Other manufactories came and went as the years went by: Viatka, Moscow, Voronezh, Pskov, Yaroslavl, Skopin. Research concerning ceramics took place at Mamantov's Abramzevo, but World War I took its toll of the work force. After that war those men who survived formed into a ceramics co-operative, and work continued on a greatly diminished scale. The State Museum of Ceramics is housed today at a mangificent and historic mansion called Kuskovo, one of the several one-time properties of the family of a London prelate, the late Father George Sheremetiev; a kindly, spiritual man who delighted in reminiscing about his one-time home of which he knew every brick.

Tiles

Ceramic tiles were primarily produced for floors, and to a smaller extent for the exteriors of buildings. Excavations of early Kievan sites have revealed fragments bearing patterns of waves and circles, some of which are at the location believed to have been the palace of the Great Princess (St.) Olga. Similar ones have been found in regions of greater habitation such as Chernigov, Novgorod, Kiev, Galich and Uglich. They were made of roughly baked clay in all shapes and sizes, and they were often glazed. In the fifteenth century production included small reddish tiles with slightly raised patterns and in the sixteenth century terra cotta showed a general improvement in quality and considerable use, sometimes for decorating the exteriors of churches.

Experiments in glazing techniques produced new and exciting effects, and the tile industry flourished. Tiles were used for decorating roofs: a sixty-foot-long roof at the Monastery of the New Jerusalem (near Moscow) was lined with tiles. They were also used for the walls and exteriors of buildings, and many of the free-standing stoves in the country were tiled. By the eighteenth century tiles had progressed from the small, roughly decorated, low-relief pieces to smooth-surfaced enameled creations, with beautifully painted patterns and a profusion of colors. Peter the Great's Summer Palace had interior walls embellished with simulated Dutch-style tiling. By the mid-nineteenth century some of the country's greatest artists, Vasnetzov and Vrubel, as well as the Mir Iskusstva artists, painted decorative tiles. But mass production took its toll. Tiles became commonplace, and by the twentieth century they all but ceased to exist as art forms.

The Lubok

The precise date of the origin of the *lubok* (woodcut) is not known, but Russia is said to have been introduced to it by the German Hanseatic merchants in the early seventeenth century. The earliest *lubki* that were produced in any quantity were at the Monastery of the Caves, in Kiev, in 1619 to 1624, although a few were already in circulation when Moscow's printing press came into being in 1564. The years 1646 and 1661 saw twenty-four plates of the Apocalypse produced at Kiev, a center for such work. A chapbook composed of twelve handpainted woodcuts, one for each month of a year, also emanated from there in 1628–9 and served as a calendar. Today it reposes in the Bodleian Library at Oxford; no doubt an intriguing story could be told as to how it got there. 1661 was the date when the first scenic woodcut was produced in Russia by Ilia the Monk; it has well defined details by means of several projections on one plane.

Lubki were seldom presented in black and white, but when a series had been completed they were sent out into the surrounding villages where peasants colored them by hand for an agreed remuneration. This arrangement provided a welcome supplement to village incomes and was part of the national *koustarnaya rabotta* (peasant arts and crafts) output. *Koustary* (village vendors) often traveled extraordinary distances peddling their wares.

Subjects for the work of the *lubochniki* were limitless: portraits of the Imperial family, victories in the field, social events, church matters, advertising and political propaganda. When political satire entered the scene of the inexpensive and easily obtainable *lubok,* censorship inevitably followed suit. The ever growing popularity of the pictorial *lubok* with the illiterate mass of the people took on a threatening aspect for the establishment, making it necessary to place production under compulsory censorship. No eighteenth-century country could tolerate a free press.

Apart from their function as broadsheets, *lubki* were also produced for advertising, as well as decorative purposes. Reproductions of icons and pictures served people who could not afford the real thing. However crude, however primitive they may have been, a great number contained charm, wit, even poetry, and a nostalgic, if naïve, simplicity; others, naturally, often went to the other extreme and were coarse and vitriolic.

A nineteenth-century art historian and writer on the subject of iconography, Dmitri Rovinsky, possessed an extraordinary collection of the national *lubok,* and wrote nine books on the subject, work which remains the premier authority to this day. He presented his entire collection to the Museum of Alexander III, presently the Russian Museum, shortly before the Revolution.

In the year 1727 copper plates replaced the wooden blocks of early woodcuts, and the nineteenth century saw lithography replace both techniques.

An interesting feature of the *lubok*'s latter day use was that many of the early ones were employed by modern architects as guides for the restoration of ancient buildings destroyed by the Germans in World War II.

The Russian *lubok* is not a particularly rare commodity and can occasionally be found by persistent collectors at such locations as old book and print shops and at auction sales.

Metal Work and the Samovar

As various art forms developed throughout Russia during the natural progress of her evolution, the art of the metalsmith did so with rather more speed than other industries. The metallurgists' production incorporates that of military requirements. When foundries began to make their appearance in specific areas, it was particularly in the regions of the Ural mountains and in the province of Tula, and it was Tula with whose name every sphere of metalwork became synonymous.

Tula's activities as a metallurgical center began in the fifteenth century, but it was not until the late seventeenth century, when Peter the Great brought various manufactories to its environs including a large munitions factory in 1711, that its renown assumed awesome proportions. That Tsar also directed many industries that specialized in the minor arts to Tula when he closed Moscow's Armory Palace workshops. Wrought and cast iron, tempered and embossed steel all came into the scope of its production. And it was at Tula that the Tsar met a blacksmith called Nikita Demidov who in 1696 initiated a cast iron business at the junction of the rivers Tulitza and Oupoi. This was the same Demidov whom Tsar Peter entrusted to manage the Neviansk workings in the Urals and to reorganize them for the State. His work pleased the Tsar; in 1726 he was ennobled. The Demidovs prospered; by the nineteenth century they owned thirty-three quarries in the Urals, including the renowned Mednoroudiansk mine where in 1835 the Demidov malachite rock was found.

Metalwork, of course, encompasses spheres in which heavy industry plays no role. In addition to armaments, vast church bells, cannon and heavy bronze doors and gates, Tula also produced delicate jewelry, ornaments and niello of the most recherché and finest quality. There were rush or taper holders, the free standing ones called *svetzy*—intricate locks and hinges, sabers, swords and rapiers, book, belt and cloak clasps, boxes and strong boxes—all came within Tula's orbit of production, as did samovars.

Samovars (the literal translation of the word means "self boiling"), although produced in Persia, Turkey and other Middle Eastern countries, are none-the-less associated primarily with Russia and the Ukraine. They were items of a tremendous output with which Tula's name became forever linked. These hot water urns have compartments for a heat source such as charcoal or wood. There were made predominently from brass, but gold and silver ones have also been found and in various, sometimes delightful, shapes and sizes. No home in Russia existed without its samovar(s), the quality of which grew into status symbols (as did the similar watermelon containers or *arbouzniki* with their compartments for crushed ice).

A little known samovar-type vehicle that had its origins in northern Russia was also Tula's production but its purpose was for cooking. The water area was divided into three compartments in which food could be heated; this utensil was popular for use during travel. Another artifact, however, preceded both these heating devices and was called a *zbitennik*. It was shaped like a kettle, and, like the samovar, it contained a heating pipe through its center. By the nineteenth century it had fallen into disuse. The writer has never seen one for sale in any country.

The above mentioned items, like flatware, were purely utilitarian and do not come under the heading of art, but, as exceptions to the rule, some splendid ones were produced, usually in minature by the country's jewelers and goldsmiths, often to specific order from the Crown Office. Like the miniature salt chair, they were often enameled and bejeweled.

The casting of massive bells is an awesome undertaking, and in mediaeval times their transport should also evoke our admiration. In the year 1730, the Empress Anna Ioanovna (the co-Tsar's daughter, 1730–40). commissioned the workmaster Ivan Motorin to cast the largest bell ever to commemorate her accession to the throne. *The Tsar Bell,* as it came to be known, was completed on November 2, 1735, but a great fire that swept through Moscow destroyed the casing it was in and toppled it, causing a large segment of it weighing some twelve tons to chip off. Sadly, the fate of this magnificent human endeavor was never to be rung. It stands today where it fell, a curiosity for the tourist. A similar fate befell the massive *Tsar Cannon* that was decorated by another workmaster, Andrei Chokral. It also stands within the Kremlin walls, and it never fired a shot. Both are produced in miniature for collectors.

The *slobadas* of Tula, Voronezh, Kostroma and Moscow were among the greater centers for bell and canon foundries, but master founders often preferred to travel great distances in order to cast large objects in situ, rather than risk transporting their creations on bad roads. Many of the bells that were ordered for churches were far too heavy for the wooden structures to support; Russian churches very seldom carried belfries. Separate bell towers were therefore constructed, usually close to the church they were made to serve, and became a feature of the Russian landscape. One such bell tower was constructed at the Monastery of the Holy Trinity (near which Zagorsk was built). It was created by the great master of Baroque, architect Count Bartolemeo Rastrelli, and, magnificent though it is, its design stands out like a sore thumb in the midst of all the traditionally Russian architecture that surrounds it.

Painted Metal

A well developed industry of painting on metal also existed in Russia, and was one of the more successful village industries. Nijhni Taiguil in the Urals was an industrious center for this work, which greatly benefited surrounding villages. A publication called *Asiatsky Vestnik* (the *Asian Informer*) stated that the Demidov workshops were running a small but prosperous and expanding business in these wares.

Trays were the most sought after items and a great many were exported. Flowers, dashing troikas, village life and folk lore were all subjects for favored decoration, in much the same manner as they were in the papier mâché industry. Toys, boxes, small busts of public figures, bears and horses were in considerable demand. Small metal icons were produced and painted, but they were not popular because chasing and enameling were the traditionally favored medium for their decoration.

Metal Icons and Crosses

Icons were produced in all shapes and sizes. Some were vast frescoes and mosaics, which took up entire walls in churches and cathedrals. Easel-painted panels ranged in size from the great ones in cathedrals that were painted on several planks of wood and "butterflied" together, right down to the minute *obrazki* that were made for wearing on chains around the neck. And there were the small, usually pocket-sized icons that were fashioned from brass, bronze copper and other alloys.

Unbreakable metal icons were favored by the great mass of the population since they were inexpensive to manufacture, cheap to buy, and, therefore, within the reach of most pockets. Such icons date from the earliest of times; ancient, pre-Tartar examples have been unearthed during recent excavations in and around Kiev. These icons are not great works of art but copies of them; historically they are of the greatest interest, and some are of very fine workmanship. A small icon representing a depiction that is known as *The Bringer of Joy to All Who Grieve* (the Virgin) was once found in an open London market by the author. Written upon yellowing paper that was glued to its back were the words *"Taken from the body of a Russian soldier at Sebastople."* Such icons were particularly favored for accompanying men to war.

The dating of metal icons is almost impossible, and many factors must be taken into consideration in order to arrive at an approximate conclusion. The subject (of the depiction), for example, can provide a clue: if the subject is a saint of the nineteenth century, then the icon cannot be of an earlier date. When examining any icon, the collector must consider the wear to which it has been subjected through cleaning and polishing over the years. Casting by the lost wax method, metal fatigue, patina (if an icon has not been over cleaned), and, strange as it may seem, a certain feel to it when handled should all be taken into consideration. Present day metallurgical expertise, of course, is an invaluable aid in resolving a problem, but since metal icons are of comparatively small commercial value, the expense for obtaining expert technical opinion is seldom worthwhile.

Metal icons were manufactured in all parts of the country especially during the eighteenth and nineteenth centuries. They came from the fifteenth-century island monastery of the Solavetskaya Lavra (or Solavki as it was known colloquially) in the White Sea, from foundries in the Ural mountains, from central Russia and from the Crimean Peninsula. The metal diptyches, triptyches and quadruptyches were especially favored. The diptyches depicted any religous subject; the triptyches were always depictions of the *Deisis*—the Prayer Icon; the three lefthand panels of the quadruptyches always tell the Christian story, often with portrayals similar to the lifecycle icons of Christ, and the righthand panel depicts four versions of the Holy Mother. The whole is surmounted by the New Testament Trinity, which dates these icons as having been manufactured in the seventeenth century or later.

In addition to the true icons of the pre-Tartar period, amulet icons also existed, evidence of the paganism that had been so difficult to eradicate during the early days of Christianity. Such icons are two sided and bear a Christian image on one side and on the obverse side very often a pagan image of Medusa with hair consisting of twelve serpents. Originating in Greek mythology, the twelve serpents represent twelve evil spirits which were thought to control twelve parts of the human body. The presence of these serpents on an icon, or protective amulet, was thought to evoke the evil spirits' pity and protection against illness. These icons were called *Zmiéviki,* or Serpentines. Wearers of them received the best from both the Christian and pagan worlds. They are rare, and seldom found on the open market.★

The traditional eight-pointed metal Orthodox cross was widely produced, often with enamel decoration. It was eight-pointed because it is considered to be a true likeness of the one upon which Christ was crucified. The central strut is self-explanatory, the upper strut bore the words "King of the Jews." The lower strut is not horizontal because when He turned to one of the robbers beside Him, the weight of His body caused the bar to move. Christ's feet are never crossed on Orthodox crucifixions as they are on those of the West.

★A permanent exhibition of metal icons and crosses may be viewed at Christ's Church College at Oxford in *The Patterson Collection.* It took some thirty years to assemble.

The Stage

Although the opera and ballet arts, and those of the dramatic stage cannot be categorized as collectible, their memorabilia most certainly can.

In addition to the decorative artists' designs, items such as maquettes for stage sets, costumes for various productions, occasional pieces from *mise en scéne,* ballet shoes that had belonged to such great dancers— Pavlova, Karsavina, Kshesinska, Nijinsky—Chaliapin's or Stanislavsky's belongings, old letters, programs and posters are all avidly collected. To locate them for purposes of purchase, yet again the beginnings of the treasure trail lie in auction rooms. Auctions take place for Russian commemorative momentos just as they do for those of the Beatles and other modern celebrities.

CHAPTER FOURTEEN

Heroic Communism

*T*he interest of all serious collectors extends beyond the pleasure of simply owning beautiful things into an absorbing desire to acquire all possible knowledge about them, to resolve all the hows and whys regarding their origins. This is the difference between the true collector and the hoarder. Post revolutionary Soviet art is a fascinating subject which can become a full time hobby. As in all things, research is the master key to knowledge, research into facts not just opinions.

Soviet art is not easily obtained because of the distances involved and the political scenario, as well as the fact that the work of the better avant-garde artists, like the Fabergé eggs, reaches astronomical prices. Luck however, plays a considerable role in collecting.

The latter day arts of Occidental Russia, when taken as a whole, show clearly their course to Socialist Realism. It was a hard road because the morass of Heroic Communism had to be negotiated; it was a period of violence, of the formation and liquidation of bodies and movements. As *parsuna* was the connecting link between the early painters of icons to the realism of the eighteenth century, so were the decorator artists and those of the avant-garde to Socialist Realism. The latter, of course, led directly to that which we now see in the arts of the U.S.S.R., art forms which are creating a considerable stir in the West today.

In chapter four we discussed the remaining vestiges of the Wanderers and the emergence of the Mir Iskusstva, the decorator artists, and the breaking away from them by the borderline artists such as Nathalia Goncharova, people who worked for both Diaghilev and the theater as well as experimenting in new areas of art. It was the work of enterprising men and women (women finally took their rightful place in the Russian arts during the late nineteenth century) who succeeded in placing contemporary Russian art on an equal footing with its equivalent in Western Europe.

On the eve of World War I, most of Russia's arts went into decline. The Imperial Ballet School admitted no new pupils during the years 1911–12; the porcelain factories gradually changed to production of purely utilitarian wares; jewelers began to produce items in base metals (e.g., Fabergé's well-known copper ashtray with its centrally positioned, dramatic, black two-headed eagle). The whole of Russian life was affected by anxiety and tension; only the pictorial arts appeared to continue serenely on their ways as described in chapter four. When war finally came and the country became locked in its tremendous struggle to contain Germany's eastern military might, it was the beginning of the end for the *ancien régime*. The year 1917 saw the disgraceful peace treaty signed at Brest Litovsk between the Germans and the Bolsheviks after the short lived Provisional Government under Kerensky had been overthrown, and Russia came free to pursue her destiny.

It was a tragic destiny because despite changes, the country suffered infinitely more under Stalin than under any of the allegedly tyrannical tsars.

The Revolution brought exaltation in many quarters, and those people who chose to flee to Paris, London the Americas, were derided and maligned. A ferocious civil war developed, the Reds against the Whites. Yet in spite of these soul destroying and momentous happenings, the arts began to revive. The spirit of creativity cannot be subdued forever, particularly in the field of the non-figurative arts, many exponents of which, it should be remembered, were revolutionaries. Chagall, himself, was created Commissar for the Arts at Vitebsk by Lunacharsky. Further, El Lissitsky, a man of tremendous talent, produced a poster which incorporated the words—"Kill the Whites with a Red Blade" (Not "Beat the Whites with a Red Wedge," as the wording is incorrectly translated by some historians today; the word *bit* contains a double meaning in Russian: "to kill" or "to beat"). Political feelings were running high at that time, and it was clear where this artist's sympathies lay.

Public demonstrations in favor of the new règime were encouraged, and Lenin replaced Nicholas II on the Winter Palace's great balcony from which he and other Bolsheviks harangued the crowds. The square was hung with thousands of decorated *arshins* of canvas, the display of which was supervised by Nathan Altman who applauded the Cubist, and Constructivist paintings lauding the Revolution. Mayakovsky's poem, "Prikas Armii Iskusstva" ("An Order to the Army of the Arts") stated that the streets were the artists' brushes, the gardens their palettes. In 1925, the Commissar for Education, Lunacharsky, proclaimed that—"The people need a picture as an act of Socialism." And so it was that Socialist Realism was born on the heels of Heroic Communism (heroic communism being that of the immediate post-war era), like the proverbial phoenix, literally out of the heart of an inferno. It was a style underwritten by Lenin personally, despite the fact that initially he had encouraged the propagandist activities of the avant-gardists. But shortly and with one stroke, all the dreams and aspirations of these men and women were smashed.

"Art belongs to the people. It must have its deepest roots in the depths of the working masses. It must be understood and liked by them," said Lenin in 1923.

Socialist Realism can be described very simply: it was a reaction to art forms that were considered to be insulting to the intelligence, individual perversions encouraged by the old régime. Art had been distanced from the people and no longer understood by them. The reversion to simple, mirror-like presentation of fact was prescribed and put into effect, and everything that was termed the vulgarization of art (i.e., Symbolism) was proscribed. Creations in tune with the thinking of the day and clearly presented were the only ones that were acceptable and admired. Communism, like Fascism, rejected all experiment in art, and visual reality's flirtation with post-Impressionism, with abstractions of all kinds, came to be regarded as contemptable and degenerate. Sobriety, a form of prudery, and a Cromwellian-type iconoclasm evolved into a radical new aesthetic, with Lenin as the "pope." Pictorial fragmentation that had formed the visual language of the avant-gardists during the first two decades of the twentieth century could not, and did not survive under the Bolshevik régime.

Thus, gradually, the "ists" were dispensed with, but not without first being used to further the Cause. In 1919 an artist called Vladimir Tatlin was commissioned by the Department of Fine Arts, or IZO (which came into being in 1918 and was under the authority of *Narcompros,* the Commissariat for Peoples' Education and Enlightenment), to erect a monument in honor of the Third International. The result was an ambitious semi-mobile on the lines to those of the Eiffel Tower. It was exhibited in reduced form at the Eighth Congress of the Soviets (December 1920), at which it was applauded, but it was never later erected. Constructivism was not frowned upon by the new authorities to the extent to which other art forms were. Rodchenko's mobiles and propagandist designs were also encouraged, as was Gabo's work, but the Gli-Gli (which is not unlike the German Dada) style of Non-Sense, architectural, pictorial and physical, were peremptorily dispensed with. Tatlin's theories that certain Constructivist work represents mystical, cosmographic suggestion, are not apparent.

In Moscow, the Stroganov iconographic workshops were taken over, together with that city's School of Painting, Sculpture and Architecture, to become the Higher Technical Artistic Studios, or *Vkhutemas,* which, in 1925 became *Vkhutein,* the Higher Technical Institute. In Petrograd the Academy of Arts was closed to be reformed as the Petrograd Free Studios, or *Svomas*. Later it reverted to the *Akademia Khoudojhstvennikh Naouk,* or the Academy of Arts. *Inkhuk* came into being; it was the Institute of Artistic Culture, and its program was devised by Kandinsky personally. Movement continued until the country was reeling from change. The new broom swept very clean, but it was men such as Kandinsky who prevented it from sweeping everything into oblivion.

Vassili Kandinsky (1866–1944), a Muscovite, was a lawyer who had also trained as a painter, yet it was not until he had reached the age of thirty that he finally made the break with his profession and turned wholeheartedly to art. It could have been his long standing friendship with the Lithuanian composer-painter Mikalojus Ĉiurlionis (in Russia 1906–1911), who painted *The Sonata of the Stars,* that influenced him to make the final break. He decided to travel and went to Munich, and then on to Paris where some of his work was exhibited at the Salon. He was strongly drawn to Symbolism, and as time progressed his departure into the abstract became total. Despite his admiration of the Impressionists' *plein air* painting, and particularly of Monet (1840–1926) whose Haystack series enchanted him, his own work grew ever more visionary and obscure. He was tolerated by the new authorities because of the international respect and admiration he commanded, and for his pronounced and unquestionable brilliance.

In pre-revolutionary Russia, Kandinsky exhibited at the first *Knave of Diamonds* exhibition. In 1911 he co-founded *Der Blaue Reiter,* and in 1912 he wrote a book called *The Spiritual Art,* at a time when he became interested in the occult. Two years before Chagall, he was invited to exhibit at Berlin's Sturn Gallery, and 1912 saw the Mir Iskusstva devote an entire section of that year's exhibition to his work. In 1920 Kandinsky was working on the organization of artistic tuition programs in both Petrograd and Moscow. The violence of the Revolution and Civil War, however, disillusioned him, and he left Russia. He ended his days in Paris, not working for Diaghilev or the theater, but on his own personal fantasies which followed specific trends: Symbolism, Constructivism, and Surrealism and Fauvism, when he met Picasso and was introduced to the intriguing Spanish artist Miró (1893–1983). He never suffered poverty in emigration for his work was always in demand. And it still is.

The second of Russia's greatest exponents of the era's non-figurative arts was Kasimir Malevich (1878–1935). His origins were in the Ukraine from whence he came to Moscow to work in the studio of the esoteric Nicholas Roerikh (1874–1947), whose mysticism and moodiness did not endear him to his new and dynamic pupil during the two years that he was with him. When Malevich's creative development and imaginative designs caught the public's imagination, Larionov invited him to contribute to the Donkey's Tail and Knave of Diamonds exhibitions.* He was commissioned to do some work for Krushenikh's Futurist opera, *Victory Over the Sun* (1913), for which his design of a black and white back cloth produced considerable interest. In his opinion it was this work that first launched Suprematism. In 1915 he published his *Suprematist Manifesto*.

In spite of being an impatient man who did not suffer fools gladly, his influence on both his own and the upcoming generation of young artists was imense, and like Larionov his energy and activity were boundless. During pre-war years Malevich had produced many pictures, and it was in those years that he was at his most prolific. He believed in the principle of

---

*The coming into being of the *Ossliny Khvost* Society (Donkey's Tail) carries an amusing story: Once upon a time there lived a circus performer who owned a donkey. This donkey was taught to dip its tail into a pot of paint and then to swish it onto a clean canvas. The resulting pictures caught the imagination of the public, and began attracting substantial sums of money for their owner. Larionov heard of this story, was introduced to it and its owner, and was so taken by the proceedings that he adopted the Donkey's Tail as the name for a new society that he was forming. Since no other explanation exists for the movement's extraordinary name, there is no reason why this tale (though, possibly, not the actual unaided dipping of the tail by the donkey) should not be accepted.

This story was given to the author by the late Eugène Mollo (a Modernist painter in his own right, *Bethlehem Steel,* etc.), who worked for Diaghilev and was a personal friend of both Larionov and Goncharova. He became a collector and expert on Russian militaria, and was recognized the world over. He was a Co-director of the Bowater Gallery, Ltd., for a while.

pure feeling, and his argument for the simplification of presentation in general brought him into conflict with many people, especially with Chagall and Tatlin. In the end he emerged as the undisputed master of the medium in which he worked. Among his masterpieces was his now-famous Black (square, circle and cross) Series, which, however, he did not exhibit until 1915—a foible of his was that he often did not show his work until a good time after its completion. Years 1917–18 saw his White on White Series, which, to him, was the ultimate in Suprematism for its cleanliness of pure white and barely visible outlines. But it was his dynamic *Yellow Quadrilateral on White* (1916–17) which was his most impressive work. He became interested in Architectonics, and began designing pottery in the various styles in which he worked. Most importantly he resorted to teaching, first at Vitebsk (where he replaced Chagall), later in Leningrad. It should be added that his realistic portraiture, such as a painting of his brother (1933), was of the first order. Unlike Kandinsky and Chagall, he never left Russia, where he died in 1935.

In 1989 an exhibition called 100 Years of Russian Art, 1889–1989, toured Britain in exactly the same way as the Wanderers (the *Peredvijhniki*), and/or their work once toured Russia. The paintings, engravings and Soviet porcelain shown was selected from private owners in the U.S.S.R. by the Director of the Museum of Modern Art (Oxford), David Elliott, and Valerii Dudakov, a Soviet art historian. The exhibition was of considerable importance since it presented the arts of Russia to many Britishers for the first time. It was an event that would have been unheard of a few years before.

It is with sadness that I have to say that I found it disappointing. It was top heavy with work by the *avant-garde* artists which, after all, was a very small section of the country's arts and was extant for only a short time although it did, of course, produce great talent. It also lacked the works of many of the greater artists who lived in the years the exhibition's title describes, and very little of that which was presented was of their better work. Where was Repin? Where were Maliavine's multitudes of colorful and delightful peasant women? Shishkin's glades and trees? Indeed, where were Nesterov, the Macovsky brothers, Vereshchagin, Yaroshenko, the Polienovs, Loucomsky and Dobujhinsky, Bilibin's delicious illustrations of fairy tales, Sverchkov's hunts and horses, Sviatoslavsky, Prianishnikov and the innumerable others?

The exhibition's catalogue was beautifully presented. In its Foreword, however, David Elliot makes the now-to-be-expected reference to Russia's pre-Revolutionary era: "At the end of the nineteenth century the structure of Russian society seemed barely to have emerged from the shadows of the Middle Ages." This type of uninformed, sweeping statement Valerrii Dudakov (perhaps intentionally) does not make, leaving it to the Britisher to cast aspersions. His Introduction is exactly what was to have been expected. It is knowledgeable, rational, sincere if somewhat naïve. He talks about the various magnificent collections in the Soviet Union which consist of pictures, etc., that were presented to the museums and galleries. He forgets, or perhaps prefers not to mention, that many of them were forcibly seized and not presented, and their owners if they protested too strongly were detained. Mr. Dudakov's discussion of post-revolutionary art and the power of the poster, if slanted to the party line, is nevertheless of great interest.

In spite of these remarks of mine, I am pleased to have had the opportunity to view this exhibition, for some of the exhibits were of the first water. The three pictures by Zinaida Seribriakova were of considerable quality; the works of Malevich, though scattered through the rooms, were splendid to behold but none of his Suprematist work was to be seen; one of Russia's greatest landscape artists, Levitan, was represented by some dismal huts; Tatlin's latter-day work was represented by a sombre *Bouquet* (1940), in which none of his exuberance was detectable. The catalogue claims that this exhibition was not tendentious. Politically, on the whole, it was not, but tuitionally it could not avoid being so. And this is the reason for most of my above remarks.

The porcelain, other than a delightful group of *Europa and the Bull* by

Serov, was predominently propaganda ware, carrying titles such as *Long Live the Third International,* and some Suprematist items: it was of interest for what it was.

One further point must be made: the dismissal of academic art by Malevich, Marionov or Pirosmanishvilli (the latter part of his name is omitted in the catalog) which the catalogue reports, provides an overall impression that this was so by most Russian artists of that era. The contrary is fact. By the early twentieth century the Academy of Arts had made its peace with the Wanderers, and Academism is seen in many Russian artists' work at that time, including in that of some of the designer artists. Their work is also barely represented at this exhibition.

It is safe to say that the third man who dominated the early revolutionary era of the avant-garde artists was Vladimir Efgrafovich Tatlin (1885–1953), a protégé of Goncharova and Larionov. His artistic education consisted of a course at the Penza School of Art, and at the School of Painting, Architecture and Sculpture in Moscow (1909–11). Almost from the first, Tatlin was drawn to Constructivist creations; he experimented with glass, treen, metal and stone, into which he introduced photography and lettering. A preoccupation with machines and industrial activities absorbed his thinking, and lofty theories regarding the effect of engineers and engineering on artistic thought prevented his considerable talents from taking more spiritual directions. He was not above resorting to fisticuffs with people who ventured to protest his theories, especially Malaevich, whom he greatly admired. Tatlin's corner reliefs, montages and photo-montages, even his paintings, became totally Constructivist and he dispensed with picture frames, claiming they detracted from space, and thereby from time. He moved far from his early, more fluid style of painting. His delightful designs for *The Emperor Maximillion and His Son Adolf* (1911) and *A Life for the Tsar* (1913) could have been painted by a different hand. He also designed furniture.

In 1917 Tatlin decorated the Café Pittoresque in a Moscow basement with Rodchenko and a badly wounded soldier-artist, Yakoulov. After he created plans and miniatures for his proposed *Monument to the Third International* (1920), Tatlin worked for a while at the Kiev Art School (1925–7), then at Vkhutein in Moscow (1927–30) as an instructor, where he also acted as the Director of the ceramic faculty. (Vkhutein was liquidated in 1931.) He then designed for a theater in the Ukraine, but returned eventually to Leningrad for the rest of his life to concentrate on aerial structures and utilitarian artifacts which he assembled for artistic consumption. Latterly his work reverted to somewhat somber, realistic painting. Like Malevich, he never left Russia where he died in 1953.★

In the early twentieth century Russian women artists rose up out of the shadows of years of oblivion. Vera Polienova and Nathalia Goncharova were the first ones to emerge, then Iakunchekova and Oustromova-Lebedeva followed, but, only Goncharova was avant-gardist, as was Olga Rosanova (1886–1918) who was also a political artist and an illustrator.

Lioubov Popova (1889–1924) studied with Metzinger and Tatlin and often worked in the latter's studio. She was a Cubo-Futurist artist (the *Violin*), an exponent of Suprematism and Architectonics, and exhibited at the Knave of Diamonds; she also taught at Svomas. Another of the era's great female artists was Alexandra Exter (1884–1949), who was a Futurist and abstract artist of considerable talent, a one-time pupil of Tairov at the Kamerny Theatre in Moscow (which became the Jewish Theatre with Mark Chagall as its Artistic Director). She traveled extensively and became acquainted with many leading Modernists—Braque, Picasso, Apollinaire and others. She finally emigrated to Paris in 1924.

★The progress in the work of the American artist, Jackson Pollock (1912–56), although his lifespan ran almost parallel with that of Vladimir Tatlin whom he never met, is somewhat reminiscent of the Russian's. Both their early work bordered on the conventions of Romantic Realism, but it quickly moved into the world of Modernism and the disciplines of Cubism, and then on to their own worlds of abstract conceptions.

They both rejected frames and easels, Pollock to a smaller extent than Tatlin. Pollock stated that easel-painting was a dying form. In Russia it was not until the days of Yuri Pimmennov and Alexandre Deineka and the OST movement that easel-painting recovered its status among the avant-garde.

Other important women were Puni's wife, Bogoslavskaya, Nadejhda Udalzova, Zinaida Kobletskaya, etc. Some of these produced unique work for the renowned Russian puppet theater, which had been an extremely popular art form in the pre-revolutionary years, and continues to be so in the Soviet Union today. "Marionettes are made in the image of man, but this resemblance is extremely conventional, and its visual means of expression is quite unique. . . . The marionette has its own language of gesture into which it translates human emotion. Its creativity is an artistic synthesis," as stated by my aunt, Lioubov Vassilievna Shaporina-Yakovleva in her memoirs.[*]

The arts of post-revolutionary Russia are best illustrated by the work of the pictorial artists. Their work extended into many areas of production: into furniture, puppetry, sculpture and woodwork, architecture, engraving, and also into porcelain production, the decoration of which became, if for a short while, almost totally political, hence, "propaganda porcelain." Iconography, of course, having been termed "the opium of the people" by Lenin, was non-existent. People hid icons to ensure their preservation, a brave thing to do because if searched and icons were found, deportation, or worse, often followed. With the coming of Socialist Realism a neo-Academic style developed (there was no Wanderers school of painting as such), but any departure into pictorial fragmentation was met with serious displeasure and, very often, with dire consequences.

World War II was a total war for the Russians with the German forces reaching the outskirts of Moscow, and penetrating deep into southern territories. Its conclusion brought a return of Stalin's reign of terror, in addition to the massive reparations that were desperately required, so there was neither time nor inclination for art, although certain schools continued to function. A dense pall of obscurity engulfs those years. The iron curtain well and truly descended.

---

[*]Cited by Nathalia Smirnova. *Soveteski Teatr Kukol*. Page 100 from the manuscript of L. V. Shaporina—Yakovleva's memoirs, and in personal conversation with her. She was the widow of the composer of the opera *Dekabrist (The Decembrist),* and other similar work. She never left Russia, survived the horrific siege of Leningrad, and died 1966.

With Stalin's demise and those of his successors, a gradual relaxation between Eastern and Western Europe began to develop. More and more tourists found their ways into the U.S.S.R. The art centers, churches and monasteries resounded with extraneous languages, interests kindled, and all things were, and are being accompanied by an ever growing co-operation, even enthusiasm. Visiting Russia has become fashionable, as well as almost *de rigeur* for the serious collector or investor, as well as for dealers in Rossika.

Western auction gallery representatives visit the Soviet Union regularly touting for trade. Sothebys recently held an extremely successful sale in Moscow, with prices that had been expected to go into the hundreds, going into the thousands, for pictures by unknown Soviet artists. It was a cause of considerable surprise to many people, but, upon reflection, and judging by past history, the amount of untapped and undiscovered talent that must lie behind that hopefully corroding curtain must be immense.

Among the Soviet artists whose names first emerged with the thaw were those of Pimenov and Deineka, both men of enormous talent. Yuri Pimenov (1903–77) was an activitist in various movements concerning the arts from a very early age, and was among those artists who founded the OST (the Society of Easel Painters, condemned by Tatlin and others as being passéist and smacking of pre-revolutionary decadence). In 1928, when he was about twenty-five years of age, he painted a picture called *Give to Heavy Industry* which as a *chef d'oeuvre* has become well known in the West. The subject is unprepossessing—the inside of a steel factory—but the composition, the groupings, the feel for various textures, the subdued colors are masterly. It also contains a feeling that Party Directive was never far from the painter's brush.

Alexandre Deineka (1899–1969), on the other hand, was a more diversified artist and a political activist. From an early age he involved himself in revolutionary activities, in the course of which he became a member of the October Movement; most of his early work was politicized. He received his training at the Kharkov School of Art and at the Moscow Art and Technical Studios under the guidance of two great artists, Favorsky and Petrov Vodkin. Initially he experimented with Cubism, the art of working in mosaic, some book illustrating, but the painter's brush and trowel finally won, and he went on to produce excellent, somewhat stylized depictions such as *The Defence of Petrograd* and *The Defence of Sebastople*. Eventually he painted vast murals, many of which were devoted to physical culture—sports, bathing, games. His subjects were predominantly women, though not the delicately erotic ladies of Renoir, but rather idealized, healthy, robust, *sportif* women of Soviet conception. He painted them unsentimentally, with absolute self-confidence and a refreshingly non-political approach. He was one of the greater post-revolutionary masters and one of the founder-members of OST. He taught at Moscow's *Vkhutein* (1928–30), and MIDI (1938), but the work of his students remains generally unknown. Their children's generation, however, is the one that is emerging onto the world's stage today. Deineka served as Vice President of the Academy of Arts (1962–6), where he was generally liked and certainly respected.

In London one gallery, The Winter Palace, leads the field (other than in Fabergé, for which Wartski's Kenneth Snowman remains "the Tsar") in promoting the pictorial and other arts of Russia. It has some fifteen years standing and has replaced myself on this particular scene. It is run by Nicholas Lynn, an American, whose love and devotion to his work are proverbial. He has an intriguing and vast collection of Soviet porcelain which includes a great deal of propaganda porcelain.★

New establishments that specialize in Russian Art are opening everywhere. One such gallery is now operating in a spectacularly grand manner. This is the Roy Miles Fine Paintings Ltd. Unlike Nicholas Lynn, however, Roy Miles appears to be specializing in Soviet production, almost exclusively. Despite this, a Repin that he bought in New York recently for one million dollars (which is the highest price ever to have been paid for a realist Russian painting. It was sold, he tells me, almost immediately to a Finance Company,) places him as a dealer in pre-

---

★Sadly and unexpectedly Nicholas Lynn died in June of this year, 1990. R.I.P.

revolutionary art as well. He is planning several exhibitions for the '90s.

Roy Miles often visits the Soviet Union and other East European countries to buy. In the days when I was active there was a sufficiency of Russian goods to be found in the London and Paris markets to make long-distance travel unnecessary.

The British press reports that Roy Miles has run to ground several Soviet artists of outstanding caliber, including Sergei Chepnik (b. 1953) and Andrei Gennadiev (b. 1947 in Leningrad). Chepnik's painting of *The Madhouse* is considered to be one of the Soviet Union's great pictures; it won a gold medal at the Paris Salon d'Automne. Another painting by this artist is called *The Founding of St. Petersburg*.

Peter Johnson of London's *Sunday Times* states that pictures by living Soviet artists annually increased in value by 50 percent and have grown into a £400m market. Examples range from £200 to £400,000 as Western collectors "discover" a pool of talent whose price depends more on quality than on a name-cachet incubated on Bond Street, Park Avenue or the Rue St. Honoré.

But as horizons widen, so too do the complications for the ordinary collector. Much Russian and Soviet art, hidden as it has been for the last seventy years, lacks the documentation and scholarship that guards against counterfeiting in the sophisticated Western markets. The plunder of the East may not be without its sting for the amateur and the unwary.

Nowadays a casual saunter through London's streets would lead to an encounter with a Russian painting or two prominently displayed, though not so yet in the case in major American cities. Sadly, a visit to any museum in Britain would provide very little of serious interest, other than some excellent examples of the avant-garde and decorators work, collections of commemorative coins, silver, posters, an occasional bronze, a few icons here and there, and some porcelain. Regretably the same seems to be true of the more important museums in the United States of America. Although there exist several magnificent collections of the work of Fabergé and of the avant-gardists (particularly of Chagall, Tatlin, Malevich, Popova, Exter, Kandinsky, Rodchenko, Larionov, Goncharova and some lesser known men and women), the only museums to possess Russian pictorial arts of any consequence are Hillwood and the Virginia Museum of Fine Arts.

On October 5, 1989, Christies (London) auction rooms conducted a sale of Imperial and post-revolutionary Russian art. It was put together by Alica Milica Ilich and her team, and it will probably be some time before another collection of such excellence will be so presented. The catalog in itself, is a work of art. The prices were high, but not too high: Russian art has only just appeared on the West's horizon, and it will be a good decade or two before it is correctly assessed. The icon of St. Nicholas, for example, which I mention in the Introduction was purchased for £500 some fifteen years ago, but recently fetched £5000 at auction. (At the end of this book I present a list of some of the prices that were reached at the above mentioned sale, taken from a cross section of the catalogue. I also present the results of a similar sale at Sotheby's.)

Glasnost is witnessing a return to a pre-World War I scenario because a Union of Artists has now come openly into being. It has a committee for the selection of suitable artists to its ranks, and it is said that it has already formed a preference against non-figurative arts, the latter being represented by Malevich's *Black Square*. And there are other groups. The enterprising Hermitage Group is one, and their pictures, unlike Chernishevsky's pronouncements, state *how* not *why* a picture is presented. (They paint the food queues, not why the queues are there.)

As has been said, the Soviet enigma appears to be dissolving. The past few years have witnessed contacts with various Soviet authorities and locations, including the powerful Cultural Foundation of the U.S.S.R., on the board of which sits Madame Raissa Maximovna Gorbachova. The West stands on the threshold of exploration not only of the artistic riches of Russia's dazzling past, but also of the work of a vast coterie of contemporary artistic talent.

In Conclusion

All the artifacts that have been described in this work, within reason, can be obtained in the West. I know this to be so because, in the course of my activities in the United Kingdom's commercial world of art, I have handled most of them. Locating them is a question of perseverence and of love for one's subject. It is fun, engrossing, and, as is most collecting these days, lucrative—providing that one knows what one is doing.

I wish my reader luck, and, since to my knowledge no other book exists on collecting Russian art and antiques, I hope that mine will be of help.

M.B.

Result of Sale Prices (Sotheby's, 5th April, 1990, London)

Lot   6. *Study of Trees.* Oil on canvas. Isaac Levitan.   £2090.00

Lot 35. *A Galloping Winter Troika.* Oil on canvas. Nikolai Sverchkov.
£13,200.00

Lot 68. *The Boudoir of the Empress Maria Alexandrovna (1824–80) at Gatchina.* Water colour over pencil. Oval, 26½ × 32". Alexandre Benois.
£7480.00.

Lot 101. *A Portrait of the Emperor Paul.* Signed by Stepan Shchukin on reverse, and dated 1797. An excellent and most important portrait. 22¾ × 16¼".   £39,600.00

Lot 188. A massive gilt-metal mounted porcelain urn, probably Imperial Porcelain Factory, carrying s-shaped, reeded and foliate handles. Unmarked. Height 76.3cm, 30".   £20,900.00

Lot 191. A Soviet porcelain Propoganda Plate, inscribed *The International,* 1921. Imperial Porcelain Factory Green under glaze mark, with a blue overglaze Soviet hammer and sickle mark and the date, 1921. A blue asterisk is incorporated for the artist Elizavetta Potapova. Diameter 10½".   £1760,00

Lot 194. A Soviet Propoganda Plate after a design by Sergei Chekhonin (the Director of the newly named State Porcelain Factory). 9¼".
£3740,00

Lot 199. A Walrus Ivory *Laretz* (casket). Northern seaboard. Height 8¼".   £1980.00

Lot 203. A rare silver and enamel bowl. Possibly Solovychgodsk where the Stroganov family established an art center following their escape from the Novgorodian troubles in the 16th century. A similar bowl is located at the British Museum. Diameter 6″.   £6600,00

Lot 204. A set of eighty four black and white plates, quarto, spine damaged. *Mobilier et Décoration des Anciens Palais Impériaux (Musees du Peuple).* G. K. Loukomsky. Loukomsky sometimes signed his name with the 'ski' ending which was, of course, incorrect since he was a Russian and not a Pole.   £935,00

Lot 207. A shallow Parcel-gilt double handled charka. Diameter 3″. 'Apparently unmarked'.   £3740,00

Lot 240. A massive malachite and gilt desk ink-well. By Khlebnikov, Moscow. Maker's mark and Imperial warrant. Width 19¾″.   £8250,00

Lot 258. A gold mounted enamel easter egg. ⅞″. Fabergé.   £1320,00.

Lot 260. A Fabergé vesta case. By F. Afanassiev, S.P.B. In fitted wood case, the silk-lining stamped with K. Faberge.   £2640.00

Lot 266. A Fabergé wood and enamel photograph frame, H. Armfelt workmaster. SPB. Height 8¼″.   £14,300,00

Lot 269. A large (34½″) bronze bust of *Mephistophelese* by Mark Matveievich Antakolsky.   £18,700.00

Lot 279. A 17th century Russian icon of the Deisis. Some 19th century repair. 27×23.5 cm.   £2200,00

Lot 308. *The Dormition.* Novgorod, c.1480. 54.5×42 cm.   £132,000,00

Lot 322. *The Crucifixion,* 19th century, the panel inlaid with a brass and blue enamel cross. 31×26.5 cm.   £1430,00

Result of Sale Prices (Christie's, 5th October, 1989, London)

Lot 22. A small rectangular *trompe l'oeil* cigarette-box with engraved tax bands and a monogram. Maker's mark M.A. Moscow, c. 1880. 268 gr.
£1210.00

Lot 50. A gold necklace suspending fifteen coral Easter eggs graduating in size, circa 1900. Maker's initials, BA.
£2420.00

Lot 69. A mounted palisander bell-push, the spreading domed body with ribbon-tied laurel swags and beaded bands, the cabochon green stone pushpiece emanating from a chased calyx; marked Fabergé, workmaster Victor Aarne. S.P.B., c. 1880.
£1320.00

Lot 76. A shaded enamel napkin ring, decorated in muted shades of moss-green, blue, aubergine on écru ground. Fedor Rükert, Moscow 1908–1917.
£550.00

Lot 80. A shaded enamel *kovsh,* 6 inches (15 cm.) long
£1540.00

Lot 98. A rectangular niello box, the lid depicting statue of Minin and Pojharsky, etc. 3½ inches (9.5 cm.) long. Unrecorded workmaster's name in Cyrillic, A. Sh., circa 1816.
£1045.00

Lot 102. A bronze figure of a seated partly reclining Cossack, after Lanceré. 5¾ inches (12.5 cm.) long.
£770.00

Lot 117. A circular ormalu-mounted malachite box. 19th c.
£3300.00

Lot 122. A brass-mounted Karelian birch bow-fronted side cabinet, early 19th century.
£24,000

Lot 132. A cut glass flute with an opaque panel painted with the portrait of Alexander I.   £1980.00

Lot 138. Two porcelain dinner plates from the private service of H.I.M. Elizabeth I. Imperial Porcelain Factory, with overglazed black double-headed eagle and incised mark. 10 inches (25.5 cm.) diam.   £3300.00

Lot 148. A porcelain military plate, the center painted with military scene of the Bashkir Division after Vassili Charlemagne, the gilt rim decorated with ciselé Imperial eagle and tied laurel wreath, period Alexander III.
                                                              £4400.00

Lot 149. A pair of plates from the banqueting service of the Imperial Order of St. Andrew, Gardner Factory. 9¾ inches (24.7 cm.) diam.
                                                              £4950.00

Lot 221. A portrait of the poet, Alexandr Pushkin by Petr Sokolov (1791–1848). Pencil, pen and black ink and water-color heightened with white on paper.   £44,000.00

Lot 239. *Return from the Market* by Nikolai Sverchkov (1817–98), oil on canvas, 30¾ × 17¼ inches (78.2 × 120 cm.)   £26,400.00

Lot 242. *Ships in a Stormy Sea,* by Ivan Aivazovsky (1817–1900), 32 × 45 inches (81 × 116 cm.).   £41,000.00

Lot 301. Bakst. *Daphnis and Cloé*. Pencil and water-color on paper. Signed and dated 1912. 10 × 8 inches (27 × 22.6).   £12,100.00

Lot 349. A Soviet porcelain mug with the head of Lenin in sepia, after N. Altman. Lomonosov Porcelain Factory, c.1926.   £1100.00

Lot 357. A Soviet porcelain propaganda plate   £7700.00

Lot 366. A Soviet porcelain Suprematist teapot   £3300.00

Lot 422. *Paris Bridges* by Alexandra Exter (1884–1949)   £330,000.00

The rate of exchange calculated @ $1.60/100 to the British £1.

Selected Bibliography

Alpatov, M.V. *Tresors de l'art Russe*. 1966.

Alpatov, M.V. *Art Treasures of the Kremlin* (in Russian). 1956.

Berton, K. *Moscow*. USA: 1978.

Bowater, M. *Russian Decorative Art*. London: 1990.

Bunt, C.G.E. *Russian Art from Scyths to Soviets*. London: 1946.

Chamot, M. *Goncharova*. London: 1979.

Fitzlyon, K. and T. Browning, *Before the Revolution*. U.K.: 1977.

Gershenson and Chegodaieva. *Levitsky* (in Russian). Moscow: 1964.

Grabar, I. *The History of Russian Art,* 7 volumes, 7th missing (in Russian). St. Petersburg: 1909–16.

Gray, C. *The Russian Experiment in Art, 1863–1922*. London: 1922.

Haftmann, W. *Chagall*. New York.

Hare, R. *The Arts and Artists of Russia*. London: 1965.

Haskell, A. *Diaghilev, His Artistic and Private Life*. London: 1935.

Heard Hamilton, G. *The Art and Architecture of Russia*. London: 1975.

Kargar, M.K. *Ancient Kiev* (in Russian). USSR.

Kagar, M.K. *Monumental Painting in Russian Art, 11th–15th Centuries*. 1952.

Kondakov, N.P. *The Russian Icon*. Translated from German, and abridged: Oxford: 1927.

Korostin, A.F. and E.I. Smirnova. *Eighteenth Century Russian Engravings* (in Russian). Leningrad.

Lazarev. V. *Iskusstva Novgoroda*. Moscow: 1947.

Lazarev. V. *Old Russian Murals and Mosaic*. London: 1966.

Lebedev, A. *The Itinerants*. USSR: 1982.

Lenin, V.I. *Lenin on Religion*. Translated into English: London.

Likhachev, N.P. *Material for the History of Russian Icon Painting* (in Russian). St. Petersbrug: 1906.

Loucomsky, G.K. *L'Art Decoratif Russe*. Paris: 1966.

Loucomsky, G.K. *Charles Cameron*. London: 1943.

Loucomsky, G.K. *History of Modern Russian Art*. London: 1943.

Marsdon, C. *Palmyra of the North*. London.

Mashkovzev, N. *Orest Kiprensky*. Moscow, 1944.

Mephishville, R. and Tsintsadze. *The Arts of Ancient Georgia*. London.

Muratov, P. *Les Icones Russes*. Paris: 1927.

Nekrassova, M.A. *Palekh*. USSR: 1984.

Ouspensky and Lossky. *The Meaning of Icons*. Translated from Russian by G.E.H. Palmer and E. Kadloubovsky: USA: 1952.

Pares, Sir B. *History of Russia*. London: 1931.

Payne, R. and Romanoff, N. *Ivan the Terrible*. USA: 1975.

Pronin A. and B. *Russian Folk Arts*. USA, 1975.

Reau, L. *L'Art Russe sous Pierre le Grand à nos Jours*. Paris: 1922.

Shcherbatov, Prince. *An Artist in Vanished Russia* (in Russian). Paris.

Shelkovnikov. B.A. *Russian Glass of the 18th Century*. London: 1960.

Shoumkina, A. *Ancient Rus*. Paris: 1971.

Sidamon Eristov Prss, A. and N. Chabelskoy. *Peasant Art in Russia*. USA.

Sitwell, S. *Valse des Fleures*. London.

Snowman, K. *Carl Fabergé*. London: 1979.

Stewart, G. *The White Armies of Russia*. London: 1933.

Struve, G. P. *Soviet Russian Literature*. USA: 1951.

Stuart, J. *Ikons*. London: 1975.

Talbot Rice, D. *Byzantine Art*. London: 1935.

Talbot Rice, T.. *A Concise History of Russian Art*. London: 1963.

Tarsaidze, A. *Katya, Wife Before God*. USA: 1970.

Trofimova, T. *Russian Watercolor* (in Russian). Moscow: 1966.

Voronkhina, A.N. *Malachite in the Hermitage Collection*. USSR: 1963.

Ware, T. (Father Kalistos). *The Orthodox Church*. UK: 1963.

Wernher and Hoftmann. *Chagall*. USA.

Yaremich, S. *M.A. Vroubel*. Moscow, 1911.

Index